grouch-ish

A SNOWED-IN, SILVER FOX HOLIDAY ROMANCE.

L.B. DUNBAR

www.lbdunbar.com

L.B. Dunbar
ROMANCE. FOR SEXY SILVER FOX LOVERS.

Other Books by L.B. Dunbar

<u>Sterling Falls</u>
Sterling Heat
Sterling Brick
Sterling Streak
Sterling Clay
Sterling Fight
Sterling Touch
Sterling Stone

<u>Chicago Anchors</u>
Elevator Pitch
Catch the Kiss

<u>*Parentmoon*</u>

<u>Holiday Hotties (Christmas novellas)</u>
Scrooge-ish
Naughty-ish
Grouch-ish
Elf-ish

<u>Road Trips & Romance</u>
Hauling Ashe
Merging Wright
Rhode Trip

<u>Lakeside Cottage</u>
Living at 40
Loving at 40
Learning at 40
Letting Go at 40

<u>Silver Foxes of Blue Ridge</u>
Silver Brewer
Silver Player
Silver Mayor
Silver Biker

L.B. DUNBAR

<u>Sexy Silver Fox Collection</u>
After Care
Midlife Crisis
Restored Dreams
Second Chance
Wine&Dine

<u>Collision novellas</u>
Collide
Caught

<u>*The Sex Education of M.E.*</u>

<u>The Heart Collection</u>
Speak from the Heart
Read with your Heart
Look with your Heart
Fight from the Heart
View with your Heart

A Heart Collection Spin-off
<u>*The Heart Remembers*</u>

BOOKS IN OTHER AUTHOR WORLDS
<u>Smartypants Romance (an imprint of Penny Reid)</u>
Love in Due Time
Love in Deed
Love in a Pickle

<u>The World of True North (an imprint of Sarina Bowen)</u>
Cowboy
Studfinder

clarification

In researching "The Twelve Days of Christmas", I had no idea about the religious symbolism behind each day, and I'm someone who had sixteen years (grade school, high school, and college) in Catholic education. As the saying goes, I was today years old (which was fifty-four at the time of writing) when I learned the true meaning behind each day in the dozen and the gifts given by a true love.

This romance is not that song.
Quite notably, it is the opposite of the spiritual meaning in those classic lyrics.

It's a fun take on twelve days of forced proximity that plays off increasing gifts or tasks needed to redeem our hero and open the heart of our heroine. It's parody and pleasure with no malicious intent toward the original twelve-day carol.

This story also takes place during the traditional twelve days of Christmas from December 26 to January 6, another religiously symbolic date, and marking the end of the Christmas season.

In this romance, it's only the beginning for Brock and Pear.

Take it all with a grain of salt. Or rather, a snowball of love.

warning

While many consider the holidays the most wonderful time of the year; others find it the loneliest. If you or someone you know is struggling in a way that might result in physical harm, please seek help.

day 1

a firebird among pear trees

December 26

chapter 1

[Brock]

"I'm giving you a leave of absence."

What? My battalion captain could not be serious but his narrowed eyes glaring at me from the other side of his firehouse office desk suggest he is one hundred percent in earnest.

"Is this a joke?" I still counter.

"You have a bad attitude."

I do not have a fucking bad attitude.

"You're angry."

I don't have anything to be angry about.

"Since the divorce . . ."

Okay, there is that.

"And your kids headed out."

Well, there is *not* that.

"And then Nat."

What the fuck? Now that's just hitting below the belt.

"You need a break."

"What I need is to work," I bark, possibly giving evidence of that attitude he's mentioning.

"It's the holidays." Battalion Captain Frank Klaus, rhymes with louse, continues.

Aw fuck. No . . .

"And, effective immediately, you're on furlough until January 6."

"Why the sixth?" That's longer than the holidays. Why a furlough at all? It was one simple punch. We were horsing around. Dane and I are like that. Until he had to go shooting off his mouth, and bring up my ex-wife, who is marrying my former best buddy during said holidays.

I wasn't angry. The divorce was roughly five years ago. I got nothing to be angry about. She made her bed, which happened to be our bed, that we'd slept in together, in our house, that we owned together.

Where I found her with Kenny.

Fucking Kenny of all people.

I swipe a hand over my short hair where new gray flecks appear every other day with all the changes in my life. Melissa leaving. Nick and Eleanor off to college. My younger brother Zebb getting married and having another kid in his forties.

Fuck me. That would be the last thing I'd want. I already have two kids. Two amazing kids. Top of Santa's list for good kids.

But it's been strange with them both gone. The house too empty. The nights too quiet.

Working for the Chicago Fire Department—CFD—has been my salvation. Work, and a glass or two of Jameson whiskey every night. Best Irish whiskey there is.

Maybe it was more than two glasses at O'Malley's the other night. And maybe Dane and I got into that row in public. And maybe I shouldn't have punched him for running his mouth.

"Because the sixth works with the retreat I'm sending you on."

"What retreat?" The bite in my tone is as strong as my bark. I'm not going on a fucking retreat, holding hands and singing *cum-bye-eye* or whatever type of song with a bunch of dudes.

"Mine."

"Aw, Cap." He has got to be kidding me. I've heard about his retreats. Taking guys into the woods near a place he owns in Michigan. What happens on those retreats stays at those retreats but most men (and women) who Cap takes on them come back changed.

I don't want to change. I'm happy being my grouchy, grumpy, forty-five-year-old self.

Brock Madison Scroggs does not need reformation.

I'm perfectly fine as I am.

"Two weeks of nothing but fresh air and quiet woods. You need time to reflect. Re-evaluate. Re-group. And change your fucking attitude." Cap points in my direction with a thick finger suggesting he isn't taking any more arguments from me.

The physical altercation is my second strike on a record that's had some shaky moments over the years.

I'm loud, opinionated, and sometimes my mouth gets ahead of my brain. On this particular occasion, my hand reacted first.

"Cap."

"You report December twenty-sixth, nine a.m. sharp. Account for the time zone difference."

"Cap."

Frank sighs heavily, leaning forward in his chair. "Brock. I like you. You know I like you."

"Cap." I'm already shaking my head. He's a touchy-feely kind of guy and I hate that about him.

Okay, I don't hate it, but strongly dislike it. Feelings make me itchy. Melissa used to say I didn't have any emotions. Yes, I did. I'd loved her and she'd cheated on me. Now, I hate her. Simple.

"I don't want to lose you, Brock."

"I'm not going anywhere." Swallowing hard, my voice softens as much as the rugged tenor allows. I'm sitting right here, taking this crap, because I don't want to leave the department. It's all I have.

"You are if you can't get your hotheadedness under control."

"I'm not hotheaded." The rise in my voice followed by the tip of his eyebrow confirms his point.

Okay, maybe I'm a little hot.

Warm.

Just mediocre temperature.

I'd say room temp but sometimes I have trouble reading a room. Like the fact Dane was joking and I'd had too much to drink the other night. The annual Snowball's Chance fundraiser was held, as it is every year, at O'Malley's and those of us without wives and girlfriends lingered late.

Pfft. Half these guys weren't heroes. Didn't know what it meant to be heroic. To race into a blazing inferno desperate to find your buddy and then watching him fall through a hidden air shaft, breaking him in half and incinerating him.

The vision comes fast and furious, and out of nowhere like it always does. The department shrink said I had PTSD. I didn't have anything that could be reduced to four letters. I wasn't sick. Another four letters. And I wasn't a fucking hero. Four more letters.

Shaking my head, rattling my brains, the memory cools like embers in a strong wind.

"It's Christmas, Cap." He doesn't need the reminder. We've had a few calls lately for live trees catching on fire, candles tipped over by cats resulting in blazing curtains, and a couple cookie-baking mishaps. Most are contained situations, but they trigger smoke detectors and set off alarms that result in us rushing to the scene.

"And it's the perfect time to evaluate your life." Cap reaches for a pencil and writes on a small pad of paper on his desk. He's old school and I could tease him about not using his phone to send me a message, but for once I keep my mouth shut.

"Here." He rips the paper from the pad and holds it out to me between his index and middle finger. "That's the address. December twenty-six at six a.m. Not a minute later."

Fa-la-la-la-*fuck* my life.

+ + +

Unfortunately, I am twelve minutes late on December twenty-sixth.

My tardiness could be attributed to any number of things.

Twinge of a headache from too much whiskey last night.

Trouble finding the freaking piece of paper with an address written on it. *Use your phone and text me!*

Turning in the wrong direction once off the highway and having to reroute.

Eventually, the sign for Paradise Farms came into view, faded and worn but surrounded by evergreen garland and a string of holiday lights which visibly twinkle on this dark and gloomy, not to mention god-awful early, morning.

Cap's farm tales are notorious. No one understands why a battalion captain for a fire department in one of the largest cities in the United States would want to own a farm in some small, rinky-dink town in southwest Michigan.

Cap claims the land is his retirement, but he doesn't appear to be jonesing to retire anytime soon. He's a pillar of physical health and still ball busting in his sixties when most guys get out of the department around the twenty-five-year mark. Not Cap.

Not gonna be me, either. I'm a lifer.

When I turn up the lane, gravel crunches beneath the tires of my Ford F-150. I immediately notice a ranch-style house and a giant faded-brown barn in the distance. My pickup truck isn't the most practical vehicle for city living. The beast would look more appropriate on this land, surrounded by trees, and there are lots of them here.

The lane I travel leads straight through rows and rows of fruit trees. Southwest Michigan is famous for apple orchards, and I remember our family visiting an orchard when the kids were little. I wasn't a farmer, God bless them. I was perfectly happy seeking fruit in the produce aisle of a grocery store. Then again, fruit wasn't always my first choice. I was a meat and potatoes guy.

The lane ends in front of a one-level house which matches the faded brown color of the barn. A long, low, covered porch runs the length of the front of the home, with a roof supported by thick square pillars in more dark wood. Garland wraps around each post and lights twinkle among the greenery. The large barn is opposite the house across the drive and another building comes into view behind it with a split rail fence beside it. I park, noticing there aren't any other vehicles present.

After scrambling around my place to find the scrap of paper Cap wrote his address on, I copied the address into my phone for the GPS.

Did I copy it wrong?

I tossed the piece of paper into the cup holder in the console of my truck, and presently lift the rumpled scrap I originally crumpled into a tight ball in my fist to double-check the address.

Nope. I have the digits and the street correct.

Plus, the Paradise Farms sign gives it away.

Hesitating another second, I glance out the side window at the weathered wood of both the house and barns. Against the heavy sky backdrop, the image is like an old black and white photo. One emanating exhaustion and melancholy. The irony isn't lost on me.

I pop open my door and step out into the crisp, cold December air. Inhaling deeply, it smells like snow with a hint of cow shit. I glance up at the sky again worried that snow might be on its way. The weather people predicted flurries but what do they know. Growing up in Chicago, I've always been taught stick around a minute, and the weather changes. Sometimes we can have all four seasons in one day. It's ridiculous.

Still, I zip up my heavy padded jacket and walk around the back of my truck, my heels crunching on the gravel drive breaks the eerie silence around me. I'm wearing an old pair of construction boots I bought when I first fixed up my house which eventually led to side jobs installing kitchens, hanging trim, or just general construction work.

A Brock of all trades. That's me.

I'm rounding the truck, turning for the front door of the home when I hear the distinct sound of feet rhythmically charging over pebbled stones. Spinning around to see who is approaching, I stall.

My mouth goes dry. My eyes go wide.

Stalking toward me is a curvaceous woman, wearing white leggings, a thick, white three-quarter zip outerwear, and running shoes. With her in a popular brand of athletic wear and those tight workout pants, she clashes with the rustic, sad barn behind her. A contrast of modern and classic. The thought is just . . . weird.

She looks like she's been out for a run—breathing fast, chest heaving, face flushed from exertion. My Neanderthal brain instantly imagines a few other scenarios where she might appear the same way.

"Who are you?" Her sharp voice is tight, almost accusatory, like she can hear my thoughts about what I'd like to do to her. She stops running a good seven feet away from me.

"Excuse me?" My tone is just as sharp.

She tugs off the ivory-colored knit mittens covering her hands and pulls the matching cap with a ball on the top off her head, and fuck me, sleek black hair tumbles down her shoulders and curls near her breasts. Her porcelain cheeks are rosy, emphasized by the exertion of running outside. She looks like a shimmery snowflake. Or a devilish delight.

She also looks pissed.

"I asked . . . Who *are* you?"

Squinting, I check her out again, top to toe, and then decide I wouldn't chase a woman with an attitude. Been there. Lost that.

"I'm Brock Scroggs. And I'm looking for Frank Klaus."

The woman stares back at me, and for a second, I wonder what's taking her so long to introduce herself or even be remotely polite.

"Okay then. I'm supposed to meet him here at Paradise Farms." I pull the slip of paper from my pocket, prepared to hold it out to her as proof I'm in the right location, although something is clearly wrong here.

She quietly mutters, "Who the hell writes something on paper?"

My head pops up and I feel the corner of my mouth tick upward. *My thoughts exactly, snowflake.*

"Anyway, I work with Cap and—"

"You missed the bus."

"What bus?"

"The bus for the retreat. I'm assuming you're one of Dad's guys needing restoration." She rolls her eyes, but I'm stuck on one word.

"Cap is your dad?"

I couldn't chase this girl even if I wanted to taste her sass on my tongue and hold those hips in my hands.

Cap would use my balls for fire extinguishing practice. My balls being the burning item.

Yeah, fuck me.

chapter 2

[Pear]

My dad.

I love the guy, but I'm still upset with him. I hadn't seen him in months, and I was looking forward to rest and relaxation on his farm. The orchard is his newest passion.

Also, restoring his flock—and I'm not meaning sheep—has been a long-standing obsession of his.

Not that I really fault him for wanting to change the culture of the fire department by rectifying wrongs done in the past, or cutting off conflict before it burns out of control, but sometimes I just need my dad. Like now.

I'm partially at fault as I wanted to surprise him for the holidays. Unannounced, I'd shown up on Christmas Eve at my dad's sister's place which is in the immediate area. Aunt Bertie was thrilled to see me. Dad, too, but he was also in shock.

"You said you couldn't make it home."

"Surprise," I'd responded weakly, noticing the concern on his weathered face.

Dad had a twelve-day mission booked with ten firefighters and police officers in need of restorative justice from December twenty-sixth through January sixth. He worked hard to get both first responder departments on board with this ancient ritual of going off into nature to find peace and perspective. Not everyone bought into the process. Some even ridiculed it, but Dad had luck at turning people around.

And from the grumpy expression mixed with the chiseled cheeks of the guy in front of me, I'd say he was Dad's newest recruit, albeit unwillingly.

At first, most participants were skeptical, hesitant, lost even. But if they wanted to keep their jobs, they followed his process for change.

Or they quit.

Or they were fired.

I knew all too well about that last option, but it wasn't my immediate concern.

Most pressing, I needed this guy to somehow connect with Dad.

The cold air rippled through the thickness of my running leggings, and I shivered. The scent of snow was in the air, which Dad always thought was a strange ability I had. To smell snow coming.

"What does snow smell like?" he'd ask me.

I didn't know how to explain it. Something fresh. Something clean. Something heavy but cozy, forcing us inside while wishing we could dance beneath it.

Dismissing the romantic thought, I glance back at the guy who works with Dad. They all kind of look the same; their age easily determined by their stature.

However, this man looks rather buff, and a bit formidable, in his heavy canvas jacket and worn construction boots. His hair is still dark on top but flecks of gray, like a dusting of snow, settle in the mix. The whiteness is heaviest near his ears. His jaw is covered in fresh scruff, like he recently shaved, but the facial hair grows back quickly. He has city-guy etched into his stiff cheeks and hard chin. His eyes are dark like coal but also sad, like a scared little boy resided inside him.

Silly, I know. Dad's woo-woo rubs off on me sometimes.

"Let me just call Dad." With my mittens in one hand, I unzip the pocket in my heavy running jacket and retrieve my phone. With a quick glance at Brock, as he said his name was, I watch him slip his hands into his pockets and hunch his shoulders upward to ward off the cold.

I wasn't a fan of standing out here with the temperature dropping and a cold sweat congealing on my skin, but I also wasn't about to let a stranger enter the house. He might be able to overtake me with his size, but I'd have some speed on him in my runners compared to his boots. Not that I planned to run or him to chase me. Just being cautious in the modern era as a single woman on a secluded farm with a big man before me.

As the call rings, I pray Dad will answer. He couldn't have gotten far yet. Maybe he could turn around and pick Brock up. Worst case, he sends Brock home.

Brock turns his head and looks off in the distance. Not much to see other than a lane leading away from the house and further into the orchards. I observe his profile. That strong chin. A solid nose. Lush lips pursing.

"Pear?"

"Hey, Dad." My voice is too high, as if caught doing something I shouldn't be doing, like ogling one of Dad's men. Clearing my throat, I tease, "I've got a stray here."

Brock's attention turns back to me, and our eyes meet for only a second. A zing rips up my center at that momentarily connection. Like the flick of a lighter, that sparks but doesn't catch. The heat passes.

Quickly, I glance at the ground and toe my right foot through the gravel. "Want to come back and get him?"

"I can't, honey. If we don't stay on the road, we'll miss this window in the weather, and I want to reach camp before snow hits."

Lifting my head, I gaze up at the sky again. With a squint, I take in the heavy clouds. "Want me to send him home?"

I don't know why I'm asking. Of course, I'll send him home. He can't stay here. I just didn't want to be the bearer of bad news.

With my question to Dad, I hear the distinct crush of gravel and drop my gaze once more to Brock. He's taken a few steps closer to me. His dark eyes are wide.

Let me talk to him, he mouths, holding out a thick hand, pink from the heat of his pocket but rugged and chapped looking.

"He wants to talk to you," I say, preparing to hand the phone to Brock.

But my dad quickly retorts, "No."

"What?" Keeping my eyes on Brock, I hold my breath. Why am I playing middleman here?

A pause sits heavily between Dad and me before my nickname fills the line again. "Pear."

I recognize that tone. That distinguished and stomach-sickening cadence where my dad is about to tell me something I won't like.

Mommy's gone, baby.

The particular sound is branded in my brain.

"Dad," I counter, warning him with *my* tone that I'm not going to like whatever he suggests.

"Keep him there."

"What?" My gaze remains on Brock, who stands deer-in-headlights still while his eyes search my face. "Why?"

"He needs this."

"He needs you, Dad." Not the farm. And definitely not me. He needs Dad's retreat.

"I can't come back for him, but he's a good guy at heart. He has it in him to change. I know he does." Dad's confidence in Brock settles like a weighted chain around my ankle. "He just needs some time and perspective."

"Dad," I grit, repeating, "He needs you."

"You got this," he encourages.

However, I don't want to 'got this'. I had my own issues to contend with. "I can't give all the woo-woo advice you give, Dad."

"It's not woo-woo." Dad chuckles. "And you don't need to give him advice. Give him some tools and tell him to get to work around the place."

"Dad," I ground again, my molars clacking.

Brock steps even closer to me, holding out his big hand as if he's about to commandeer the phone from me.

"He wants to talk to you," I repeat to my father.

"You tell him he was late. I'm talked out with Brock. It's time for him to put some muscle where his mouth gets him in trouble."

I did not like the sound of that. The last thing I wanted was to spend time telling some random guy what to do on my dad's farm. Especially if he had a bad attitude or chip on his shoulder.

"And where is he supposed to stay?"

Brock is even closer now, hand over mine like he's ready to rip the phone from my grasp.

My eyes narrow, warning him with the glare. *Don't fucking touch me.*

He lifts his hand and holds it upward, palm out. Then he curls his fingers, motioning once more for me to hand him my phone.

"Put him in the barn."

"Jesus, Dad." I can't do that. The barn isn't heated and as much as I don't want Brock here, he can't stay out there.

"I'll tell him to find a hotel."

"Good luck with that. I bet most are still booked from the holiday." Christmas was only yesterday. "And I'd prefer he's at the house. I don't like you there alone."

My breath comes sharp and quick, ready to remind him he left me here. But I'm a grown-ass woman of forty-one and I can take care of myself. In fact, being alone might be exactly what *I* need for some perspective. Time to build a plan for what's next in the new year.

And the last thing I need is to be responsible for someone else.

Turning my shoulder to Brock, I whisper into the phone. "Dad, call him, and send him packing."

"Nope." Dad's quiet a second, and I hear the blinker on his miniature school bus. The one he painted dark green and plastered Paradise Farms on the side where it once read School Bus. "Tell him this is his last chance."

My mouth falls open ready to protest once more.

"Twelve days at Paradise Farms. Keep records of all he does, and I'll evaluate his progress when I return. Now I need to concentrate on the road. The snow is starting to really fall."

I glance toward the sky once more as he states, "Love you, Pear."

A light dusting of flakes tickles my cheeks and sticks to my eyelashes, as I whisper, "Love you, too."

The line goes dead, and I glance back at Brock, who is watching me. Eyes wide, hesitant yet hopeful.

Dammit.

What am I supposed to do with this guy for twelve days?

chapter 3

[Brock]

I'm pissed that Cap wouldn't talk to me. His daughter told me not to bother calling him myself as Cap doesn't answer his phone for anyone on these trips. He only answered her call because she is his daughter, and he hadn't gotten to the camp yet.

Camp. I don't remember ever camping.

"I'm Paradise, by the way." She nods stiffly as we remain outdoors, the snow softly falling around us as a precursor to something heavier. The calm before the storm, so to speak. The magic before the tragedy.

"As in Paradise Farms?" My voice is molasses-thick, almost sarcastic, but it isn't her fault I'm in this predicament.

She explained how Cap said I was late. *True.*

He was done talking to me. *Harsh.*

And I could work on the farm for twelve days.

"You need to find a hotel."

"At whose expense?" I wasn't a millionaire, and I also wasn't interested in forking over money for an eleven-night stay when this wasn't a vacation. This was Cap's order.

"Not my problem."

I sigh and swipe my hand over my head. My hat is in the truck and my hair is damp. The longer I stand out here, the colder I get.

"Maybe there will be another twelve-day retreat," I say more to myself than to her.

"Do you have time to wait?"

My eyes latch onto hers again. *Fuck, she's pretty.* That dark hair contrasts with her cerulean eyes reminding me of the bright blue holiday lights twinkling along houses this time of year.

"I doubt it." Again, said more to me than her.

Cap must really be at the end of his rope because no man gets left behind is a motto of our department. I realize I was late, but he could have turned around. He couldn't have gotten very far in twenty minutes. Or he could have given me the address and I'd drive there myself. Still, his actions said it all.

He wasn't coming back. He wasn't making an exception for me. Over and over again, he'd gone to the mat for me, but this was like last call at the bar. Time was closing in.

"I guess I'll call a hotel."

Noticing that I was continually talking more to myself than her, Paradise doesn't say a word. Instead, she circles around me to enter the house.

"Good luck," she calls out after I spin to watch her retreat. She wiggles her fingers in a mocking wave, enters the house and closes the door behind her without a glance back.

What the—

With the billowing snow piling up on the ground, I return to my truck, turn on the engine and search my phone for a local hotel. Nothing pops up with vacancies, not even from a motel that looks more like a rent-by-the-hour than an extended stay place.

"Shit." I glance out the front windshield where downy flakes are quickly covering the glass. "I should just go home."

I can handle Cap's wrath. Take my punishment like a man. Pay a fine or accept whatever ridiculous manual labor Cap dishes out. Scrub toilets with a toothbrush. Clean a grease trap or vacuum behind the firehouse fridge. Your basic probie work.

Still, I remain in the heat of my truck, watching the snow fall like sand in an hourglass. Cap's silent treatment hurts more than anything. It isn't like him not to want to talk. He's good at listening. He's intuitive and sharp. He knows when to back off and when to step in, but not speaking with me isn't like him.

He's really done with my shit, and I need this time, if for no other reason than to prove to Cap I'm solid. I'm strong. I'll do whatever it takes.

I've been sitting here roughly forty minutes, so I kill the ignition on my truck and push open the heavy driver's door where a cold blast smacks me in the face.

My mind is made up. I'm not leaving this farm.

Little Miss Paradise isn't going to like it.

Like a partridge in a pear tree, I'm here to stay for twelve days.

+ + +

"You what?" Paradise stands with the front door slightly ajar. The sliver allows me only a slim view of her luscious body.

"I'm staying." I pause. "Here."

The shock on her rosy face, now heated from the warmth of a roof over her head and a toasty house surrounding her goes from pink to red in an instant. Her feathers are definitely ruffled by my declaration.

"I can't find a hotel within sixty miles of this place, and I can't leave." I didn't want to beg, so I needed her to hear the resolve in my voice. I couldn't go home.

"Cap said twelve days, so I'm here for the full dozen."

Her eyes narrow. "This isn't a package of eggs. It's my house."

"Technically, it's Cap's," I counter, tilting my head and taking her in again. Those bright blue eyes. Her heated cheeks. Her cherry-red lips. That mouth looked like Christmas ribbon I wanted wrapped around my—

"Fine. Dad said you can sleep in the barn."

"What? No." I twist and glance at the large structure, worn and faded, scratched and weathered. I wasn't sleeping in a barn like a fucking animal. Turning back to her, I demand, "Just give me a room."

"No room at the inn," she mocks, before chewing at the corner of her mouth, like she's fighting a smile.

Ha. Funny. "Come on, Paradise."

She twists her lips and leans her head against the open door, eyeing me for a long, skeptical minute.

"I get it. I'm a stranger to you but I work with Cap. If I touched you, he'd have my balls."

Her head pops upright. "If you touched me, *I'd* have your balls. And I'd roast them like teeny-tiny chestnuts over an open fire."

Yikes. My gut tightens. I squeeze my thighs together.

"And I don't take orders from you either," she adds, pointing a finger at me that is oddly similar to how Cap holds his hand when his trigger is aimed at me. "I'm head elf here."

The corner of my mouth curls and I fight to control the growing grin. She's kind of cute when she's trying to be stern. She can*not* pull off scowling schoolteacher, but I'd still let her reprimand me. I'd be happy to be on her naughty list.

"Got it, snowflake," I mock, saluting her.

"I'll give you jobs around the place, take notes, and Dad can assess what you've done when he returns."

"Dad," I chide, like we're kids and she's playing mother hen, stealing my rank as top bird in this here apple orchard.

Her glare suggests I'm on thin ice with her. She could slam that door in my face, turn the lock, and stay nice and cozy inside that house. The idea makes me shiver as the cold is settling into my bones again. All the warmth I'd gained while sitting in my truck has dissipated.

"Look, I'm sorry." My tone is still too rough for the apology. "I promise I'll behave."

"I don't need you to behave—"

Our eyes lock. Her command wasn't meant to be suggestive, but I have all the suggestions for how we can misbehave together.

Then I hear my balls crackling over a roaring flame, and shiver once more.

Her gaze drops and I instantly miss the cool shock and warm glare in them. For some reason, I want her looking at me. Seeing me.

"I mean . . ." She clears her throat but doesn't fill in the space, only glances at something over my shoulder.

I'd peer behind me but I'm too afraid to look away from her. Afraid she'll close this door on me when I need this chance. I need these twelve days.

"You're welcome." Her quiet acceptance is like a warm blanket.

"Really?" I shouldn't sound so surprised, and I quickly swallow my shock and try again. "I mean, excellent." I'd love to promise she won't regret it. I'll make the top of Santa's good boy list. However, I'm not good at making promises, and I'm not about to start becoming a liar. I offer one simple truth.

"You have nothing to fear from me."

She tilts her head to the side, leaning it once more against the solid front door, holding firm to her position as keeper of the warm indoors. Another minute passes between us before she makes some mental decision, steps back and holds the door open wider.

"Somehow I doubt that," she mutters as I pass her but I don't question her meaning.

The sudden heat hits me first.

The fragrant scent of something cinnamon and sweet baking is next.

However, the sight before me is what has me tongue-tied.

The living room hosts a huge stone fireplace dressed in evergreen garland with white fairy lights twinkling amid the mix. Bright red ribbons hold the entire strand against a railroad tie-sized wooden mantel. A lumpy-looking three cushion couch faces the giant hearth while an over-stuffed red plaid chair sits in the corner. A giant Christmas tree stands beside it, bursting with ornaments and more miniature lights.

The small kitchen is open to the living space with a rectangular wooden table and six ladder-back chairs in a tight dining area. Black cabinets with a butcher block countertop in a U-formation look hand-crafted and wrap around the dining table, centering the space.

Essentially, the sight is something straight out of a magazine depicting Santa's quaint home in the North Pole.

"I guess you can sleep in Dad's room," Paradise mutters more to herself, leaving me standing just inside the front door, stomping my boot-covered feet.

"I need to grab my bag," I state, remembering my duffle is in the truck.

Paradise gives me a back-handed wave as she retreats down a hallway between the living room and kitchen.

After retrieving my bag, I quickly return inside the warm house, shucking off my jacket and helping myself to hang it on the peg rack already laden with coats and scarves. A bench rests beneath the collection, and I unlace my boots and toe them off, setting them inside an empty cubby underneath the seat.

Rubbing my hands together, I step up to the fire in the hearth that's both a hazard and magical. The space is large and deep, and while the fire is set toward the back of the open space, the flame isn't contained behind a fire-resistant mess grate or glass doors. The size and shape of this fireplace is something straight out of a Western movie.

I stand before it, hands held open and upright, mesmerized by the warm blaze and dancing heat. Being a fireman, a dichotomy exists within me. Fear and respect for flames.

I glance up at a wooden set of doors over the fireplace where a bird is painted on each panel, each almost kissing the other but separated by the sliver of a seam. The decoration looks Scandinavian and very apropos for the rest of the décor in this place. Upon closer inspection of the slightly misshapen outlines to the scratchy brush strokes within them, it looks like a child painted each bird.

Underneath one bird is written Pear. Beneath the other is Peach.

I snort. *Peach and Pear*. Cute.

"My dad loves this fireplace. It's one of the reasons he bought this farm."

Paradise's quiet voice startles me. I didn't hear her approach, nor notice that she was standing right beside me, gazing up at the painted birds as I had been doing.

"Cute birds," I quip.

Paradise huffs once. Her arms are crossed, and she can't seem to take her eyes off the birds. She's changed into a pair of loose-legged ivory pants and a matching cropped sweater that hits the top of her waistband. The material looks soft, fluffy almost, reminding me once more of a snowflake.

"Dad thinks this place was originally a one room cabin. Hence the large fireplace and open concept." She nods toward the hallway without removing her eyes from the decorated panels. "The rest of the house, which includes two bedrooms and a bathroom, was an addition."

I don't really have a response to her explanation of the blueprint, so I remain quiet, absorbing more heat and finding strange comfort in her close proximity.

"I suppose I need to feed you," she eventually says, pulling her gaze from the decoration and glancing at me. Her eyes roam the length of my body from head to toe.

Yeah, I'm fit which also means I like to eat. Meat. Potatoes. Willing women who look like snow—

"I'm not here to cater to you."

My shoulders stiffen. "I can fend for myself."

"Really? Gonna go kill an innocent reindeer for me? Or rustle us up a roast beast?"

I glare at her, uncertain how to respond to either reference. I'm no hunter. I like my meat from the freezer section.

"How about we start with what you have here? I can hit up a grocery store tomorrow." My gaze drifts to the window behind the kitchen table that offers a direct view of the heavy, wet snow, falling harder and piling higher in the drive.

"I intended to go myself." Her voice lowers, and I catch her looking in the same direction. With the way it is snowing, neither of us should be going anywhere. "But it might have to be Christmas leftovers this evening."

"That works for me." My typical breakfast of morning coffee wasn't enough today and I'm starving.

"For now, I guess I could make pancakes."

"Smells like something is already baking." Once again, the strong scent of cinnamon tickles my nose.

"Shit." Paradise rushes the few feet to the kitchen. "I almost forgot the pie."

Following her, I chuckle as she lowers the oven door and pulls out a pie sizzling on a well-used cooking sheet.

"That smells like heaven." I sniff once more and my mouth waters at the combination of something sweet and spicy filling the air.

"You think?" Her voice falters, lowering with hesitancy.

Stepping closer to her, I exaggerate inhaling, waving my hand toward my nose as if the fragrant fumes will drift faster into my olfactory senses.

"What is that?" I'm practically salivating at what I assume is an apple crumble pie, piping hot and fresh from the oven.

"A Dutch pear pie. I'm trying out a new recipe."

"You made that?" Before me on the stove top is a baked-good of perfection. Crumbles and a braided crust, not to mention the scent.

Glancing at Paradise, she chews at the corner of her mouth again. "I bake when I'm stressed."

I stand taller, realizing her stress is from my presence. I don't want to make her feel put out or uncomfortable, but I can't leave.

"I'm sorry." The words burn like hot coals as I don't say them often. How many times should I have apologized to Melissa? How often should I have said the phrase to my kids, especially my son Nick who I ride hard? Even Eleanor who never deserves my harsh tone or tough attitude. "I'm the problem, right?"

Paradise sets the potholder on the counter and straightens to face me. "I bet a real problem of yours is realizing *not* everything is about you."

"Harsh," I mumble. Too often I'm told I'm the issue. Loud-mouthed. Hot-headed. Quick-fisted. All my body parts are out of control.

"How about pie and hot chocolate for breakfast?" Paradise turns away from me, retrieving a pie cutter from a drawer and then removes two mugs in the shape of Santa heads from a mug rack.

"I'm a coffee man," I proudly admit.

"Then hot chocolate it is, as I don't know how to use the coffee maker."

Ignoring my wish, she sets a pot on the stove and fills it with milk, adds cocoa mix, and stirs. She's a regular Betty Crocker minus the apron and full of curves. I warn myself to stop staring at her ass in those form fitting white pants, which on closer inspection are made of some kind of stretchy material.

When our pie breakfast is plated and cups of hot chocolate prepared, she steps toward the table, and I rush to pull out her chair. I can't remember the last time I did such a thing for a woman. I'm not a total pig, but we aren't on a date. I don't need to impress her. Still, I can't seem to help myself.

Paradise glances up at me, her face unreadable before she takes a seat and I follow, sitting opposite her.

She lifts her holiday mug and taps it against mine without offering any toast. Then she sips her hot cocoa and closes her eyes humming. For half a second, I imagine that sound coming from those naturally cherry-colored lips as I touch her.

Then I shake my head, ridding it of the heavenly image, and focusing instead on the pie before me. With a hearty slice on my fork, I scope up the pie, and shovel it into my mouth.

"Fuck, that's hot," I mutter around a steamy mouthful, all sense of manners and decorum melted away as my mouth burns and I swallow a scorching bite of pie.

Leaning into the hard back of her chair and covering her mouth while watching me fan my hand before my open lips, Paradise chuckles. "You're kind of a mess, fireman."

"You have no idea, snowflake."

chapter 4

[Pear]

Snowflake?

Cute but not exactly complimentary. I'm a sturdy girl which means I'm more like an ice-packed snowball than a dainty snowflake. And I'm not afraid to use such as a weapon of choice, if need be, with this hot mess of a man. He could use some cooling off and I'm not just referring to his mouth where he rushed to shove pie fresh from the oven into his appropriately named pie-hole.

The alpha energy coming off him could vaporize the snow piling up outside. I bet the heat he produces works at melting panties as well, but I'm not here to have my underwear liquidized. I have my own issues at hand, and as I told him, he isn't always the focus of a situation.

"So, what's your story, Paradise?"

I pull my leg up, so my heel rests on the edge of my seat, and I wrap my arm around my bent knee. Setting my chin on the bony notch, I stare across the table at Brock.

"Not how this works, fireman. My story needs to be earned." This isn't some random first date where we speed through monotonous interview questions. What do you do? Where do you work? How long have you lived in Atlanta? Why did you move here? *Blah-blah-blah . . .*

Brock arches one of his bushy brows and watches me. His gaze flits to my lips. With the way his eyes keep roaming over my body, he's either easily distracted or vaguely interested. It's always one or the other with guys like him. The way his gaze keeps falling to my mouth I either have food on my lips or he's envisioning things I won't be doing to him. I'm not here for flesh snacks and pithy seduction.

"Let's discuss what you'll be doing."

I really thought Brock would drive away. Dad wasn't here. I was. And without my dad to keep Brock in check, I figured he'd take a free pass to leave. But something in his cold-coal eyes told me he needed this second chance. Or third. Or fourth. He needed to prove himself to Dad. Maybe even prove his worth to himself.

So, while I am surprised he returned to the door after searching for a hotel, I'd taken the time to compile a list of things Brock could do around this place. *For Dad.*

"You'll start with canning pears."

"I'll what?"

"We need the stock." I have no idea if this is true but canning pears feels appropriate for phase one of Operation Grouchy.

He glances over his shoulder, further narrowing his eyes to glare out the window behind him. The snow is really piling up and I'm not certain how he'll accomplish some of the other things on the list. Not my problem, though.

"I thought this was an apple orchard."

"Dad grows apples and pears."

Brock turns back toward me and glances down at the still-steaming slice of pie. "Did the pears in this pie come from your trees?"

"Yes. I opened a jar we had on hand, but our supply will only get us so far. We have Valentine's to contend with." Since I'm making this up as I go, I'm hopeful training from my theatre days, which peaked in high school, still work.

"Valentine's," he snorts. "A little early for the next holiday, don't you think? We haven't even reached New Year's." His nose wrinkles like he just remembered he'll be here—with me—when the new year rolls over.

Not exactly the New Year's plan I had either, buddy.

"Yes, nothing says love like a jar of pears."

Brock stares at me and it takes everything in me not to burst out laughing at the expression on his face. He doesn't know whether to believe me or tease me. While I'm trying to act as if I'm serious, who the hell would give pears to their lover? And who else is gullible enough to believe a jar of pears would be romantic?

Making an assumption, I bet Brock is a shitty gift giver, like Reggie, my ex-husband.

On our first holiday together, he gave me a George Foreman grill because he knows I like to eat. Not exactly romantic.

"Anyway, I'll set you up and—"

"I don't know anything about canning pears."

"Unfortunately for me, I'm going to have to teach you." This is the only item on the Brock-provement list that should involve me. I didn't need Brock burning down the house. However, I have no intention of holding his hand through the canning process. I'll set him up with the pears, syrup, and water, and all he'll need to do is boil and fill jars. Easy.

A memory hits. Mom in our old Chicago kitchen, following the same simple recipe. We didn't own the orchard when I was a kid. This property was acquired later by Dad.

Our dream, he'd whispered when he first brought me here.

Next comes a vision of my sister and me dancing around the kitchen table singing some silly made-up song about pears, like we were performing an ancient ritual to fruit goddesses.

A pear song from a pair of sisters.

Quickly, I brush away both memories and cut into my pie. Filling my mouth with my most recent experiment prevents me from talking, and the last thing I want to do is share more information than necessary with Brock.

Instead, I focus on the celebration in my mouth. The warmth of the filling. The flakiness of the crust in combination with the crumbles. The right combination of nutmeg, cinnamon, and Anjou pears. Closing my eyes again, I savor the flavors, the temperature, and the texture. God, I love good food, especially excellent desserts.

I'd always wanted to be a baker.

Instead, I work—*worked*—in the food industry for a top company in pre-packaged food. The product wasn't necessarily enticing, but the job had paid my bills, and I had plenty until recently.

Brock and I eat in silence. His head bows as he scarfs down the remainder of his slice, then sheepishly asks for a second. He doesn't touch his hot chocolate; instead snagging a second Santa mug from the rack and helping himself to water from the tap.

"What the hell is this?" He sputters and coughs around the mineral tang of the water while swiping the back of his hand over his mouth.

"It's well-water. There's a filter on the fridge."

"This tastes like ass."

"Really? Tasted one lately, have you?"

He smirks. "Funny."

What's your story, Brock Scroggs? What did he do to earn him a twelve-day retreat with Dad? How much trouble is he in with his department? How close is he to losing his job?

None of it should matter to me. I didn't need another deadbeat man in my life. Been there. Got rid of that, thank you very much.

After Reggie, a long time passed before I was able to go on a date. I was as selective as Santa making a list. I'd seen the good. I learned to recognize the bad. Brock seemed to straddle the line somehow. List destination to be determined, I decided, and although Christmas was only yesterday, there was no better time than the present to start making a new list for next year.

Brock had pulled out my chair. A check in the plus column.

He was a helluva good-looking man but looks didn't earn you points when behavior was the key.

Guess we'll see how naughty or nice he can be.

Even though Christmas has officially passed, the true twelve days of the season began today, on December twenty-sixth. I didn't have romantic notions of a true love gifting me a partridge in a pear tree, but it would still have been nice to spend the holidays with a partner. A couple coupling.

I almost laugh out loud at my ridiculous thought and drop my foot to the floor, leaning forward to lift my cooling hot chocolate.

Brock doesn't know what he's missing out on. This is Aunt Bertie's special recipe, complete with a dash of peppermint extract and a shot of complementary Schnapps.

There's no better comfort and joy than chocolate and alcohol.

'Tis still the season, I silently toast my new housemate, and then down the rest of my drink.

+ + +

Canning pears was a disaster for Brock. I'd set him up as promised and then excused myself for a winter's day nap. A girl shouldn't live on two hot chocolates with shots of peppermint flavored alcohol and a slice of pie, but I'd been silently toasting my sister's absence.

When I awoke, I had a text from my Dad but I was distracted when I found the kitchen was a mess; Brock was swearing; and I'm not certain a single jar was properly sealed.

Lots of disappointed lovers come Valentine's Day.

"Well," I groan, setting my hands on my hips, while chewing my lower lip, fighting a giggle at Brock's expense. He wears an apron that is slightly askew on his hips with what had to be a dribble of pear syrup down a T-shirt that hugs his chest. His hair stands up on end, possibly from sticky fingers covered in pear juice, and his facial hair has already started growing in since I'd first met him this morning.

Scanning his appearance from toe to top, I do a double take at his jaw.

I'd guess Brock to be mid-forty and nothing said yum like a dusting of gray in dark hair, but he has charred-coal coloring in his scruff, and I am poke-me-with-a-fork-and-hope-the-tines-come-out-clean done if that beard comes in more silver than ink. I'll need to keep my libido in check around all the alpha energy *and* a silvery beard.

"I told you I didn't know what I was doing," he reminds me, angry while sheepish at the same time.

Something inside me turns gooey. *Do not be soft for him.* This is no cinnamon roll standing in front of me. He's entitled, in trouble, and bad for my heart. Not that my heart wants anything to do with him, it's just that I'm a sucker for bad boys. Or rather, menacing men. With silver in their beards.

Rubbing a shaky hand across my forehead, I sigh. "I'll clean up." I shouldn't offer. This is not my responsibility. I'm here for rest and relaxation. I'm here for my own restorative retreat and I'd needed my dad.

"I've got it," Brock mutters.

"I'm worried if you have it any more than you already do, we'll be swimming in pear juice, sticking to the furniture, or torching the place."

A flame leaps up around the currently boiling over pot of water, syrup, and pear combination to accentuate my statement.

"Shit," Brock mutters, stepping toward the stove and picking up the pot by the handle with his bare hand.

He immediately drops the pot back down on the stove top, syrup sloshing over and causing the flame to sizzle once more. Hissing, he shakes out his right hand while twisting the burner dial with his left. Next, he rushes to the sink and hits the cold-water tap with the heel of his opposite hand and places the offended hand underneath the rush of water.

"Did you burn yourself?" I step forward and examine the raw skin as water pours over his tender flesh. Brock has huge hands, like a giant paw, and I shouldn't have the visions suddenly dancing in my head of those hands on me, cupping me in places that haven't been cupped in a while, palming me in other places that haven't felt the heat of another's palm in too long.

"That was so dumb," he mutters to himself, adding in additional expletives. "What a fucking idiot. This was so stupid."

"Hey!" I snap, dragging his attention to me while his hand remains underneath the spray from the faucet. "Don't talk about yourself like that. You aren't stupid."

"I didn't say *I* was stupid. *This* is stupid." He nods toward the mess.

"When someone says something is stupid, it's often not that the process is dumb, but the person doing the process feels helpless because the task is difficult. They don't understand the process and it makes them uncomfortable."

"No, I really mean this is stupid," he corrects me.

But I'm onto something. Brock is reactive when he feels out of control, and canning pears evidently made him feel that way.

He tips up his chin. "Why would you care anyway? I'm wasting your time and mine here."

I don't have an answer for the caring part but as for wasting his time . . . "Then quit and go home."

I could use the alone time and I could also do without his alpha attitude and manly mess. Pieces of pear in syrupy globs decorate the floor from stove to table, and a streak of pear juice runs down the front of the oven. Splashes of more pear sauce splatter left and right of jars scattered all over the table which was thankfully covered with an easy-to-wipe liquid resistant tablecloth, but still.

My sister and I could have done a better job at seven years old than this man at forty-five.

Brock glares a second. Those dark eyes are as black as coal, but underneath that hard surface is the potential to be a diamond. Something that might shine one day.

Only a moment passes before a flicker of light returns to his eyes, determination settling in. "I am *not* a quitter." He reaches for what appears to be a well-used dish towel and wraps his burned hand in the cloth.

"That doesn't look very sanitary." I pull open a drawer and remove a clean towel.

"I didn't cut myself. It's only a burn." Removing the towel, he shakes out his hand and examines the redness of his flesh. The skin looks raw. He might get blisters.

I reach into an upper cupboard where Dad keeps aloe vera gel for such a thing.

Cupping his wrist, I draw him to the dining table and point for him to take a seat. I pull up a chair directly in front of him and sit as well. Taking his larger hand in mine, the difference in sizes is blatant. He already has calluses beneath the burns. I lift his hand, pour the gel over his raw palm, and blow across the tender flesh, cooling any irritation. Slowly, I glance up at Brock, feeling the weight of his gaze on me. His eyes blaze, like that cold-coal glare has caught fire.

As the gel settles, he hisses before loudly quipping, "That fucking stings."

"I'm only trying to help," I remind him as my voice rises to match his.

"Again, why do you care?" His head pops up from examining his hand and I lift my eyes to answer him. Only any response gets caught in my throat once more.

While I want to tell him I don't care about him, something deep inside me hints I should.

And I have no reasonable explanation for why.

+ + +

Cleaning up Brock's pear-catastrophe took more than an hour. Afterward, I sent him to the shower, reminding him to reapply the aloe vera gel, before I started working on our dinner of leftovers. Dad's freezer is stocked but the fridge is lacking. As he hadn't planned on being here for two weeks and hadn't expected me, the basics are present but fresh foods are absent.

As I'm removing the lid from a plastic container, my nail catches and bends backwards, ripping off a portion of the nail below the bed.

"Shit." Shaking out my hand, I step toward the sink and turn on the cold water, placing my hand underneath the stream, similar to how Brock had done earlier. A slow trickle of red runs through the water.

"What happened?"

"Jesus in a manger," I shriek, having been startled by Brock's sudden appearance. Not only did I not hear him, but freshly showered Brock, standing too close to me Brock, is like an aphrodisiac Brock. He smells like winter mint and fresh snow, and looks too good in a camel-brown sweater that hugs his chest like the plastic wrapper on candy.

Which flavor is he?

Brock tenderly cups my hand beneath the cold water and examines where my nail has chipped like a broken claw.

"That's gonna hurt," he mutters.

"Well, aren't you all compassion?" Especially after I spread aloe vera gel on his hand earlier.

He doesn't reply but takes his time to add gentle pressure to my finger, watching until the water runs clean of blood. The pad of his thumb rubs up and down my finger, stroking a little longer than necessary.

"We make quite a pair, Paradise," he says still inspecting my finger while massaging the digit.

"Pear," I whisper.

"A pair, that's what I said."

"No, pear. P – E – A – R. That's what my dad calls me. Pear, short for paradise but also like the fruit."

His gaze blatantly drops to my chest before his eyes leap to meet mine. A crooked smile curls his lips. "A pair of pears."

"Don't be crass." Besides my breasts are bigger than a set of pears.

He chortles without apologizing. "We, you and me, make a pair, Pear."

"You're such a dick." Mocking my nickname when I thought I was offering a piece of myself to him sets my stomach churning. I don't know why I shared the name with him. Only my dad calls me such a thing. "Forget it. Don't use the name."

"Come on, snowflake." He chuckles. "Don't freeze me out."

Forget calling him a dick. He's worse. "Yeah, calling the fat girl a snowflake is really original."

Brock gasps, loud and strangled, while squeezing my hand more firmly. His voice drops low, almost menacing when he says, "What did you say?"

"I'm not repeating myself." I'm actually rather body-positive and have decent self-esteem, but I haven't always been like this. Reggie did a negative number on me when I was in a vulnerable state, and it took a long time to reach zero again.

"You better fucking *not* because I never want to hear you use fat in a sentence again, especially if you are referring to yourself. Which I know you were *not* just doing." The tipping of his bushy brow accentuates his point. He's not listening to this bullshit.

"The only thing I want to know about your size is how well those hips might fit in my hands. How that ass feels against my palms. And how that mouth might take my—"

"Got it." I cut him off. He's still crass, but am I turned on? Yes. Yes, I am. And that's new.

"Why the snowflake nickname then?"

Brock lowers his head, examines my finger a final time, and turns off the faucet. He grabs a paper towel to wrap around my finger for a makeshift bandage. Still holding onto my finger, he glances up at my face.

"Because when I saw you earlier, you looked like you dropped from heaven. Wearing all those layers in various shades of white, like a snowflake. And even now, wearing this fluffy sweater that looks so soft. Snowflake." His voice drops as his gaze lowers once more to my chest. He isn't leering, isn't perving. Just admiring. And while that dropping from heaven line could have been the cheesiest of pick-ups, there's a hint of sincerity in his voice that stops any mocking retort from rolling off my tongue.

Instead, my nipples harden within my bra while my face heats.

Brock lowers his head and presses a kiss to the tip of my paper-towel wrapped finger, like kissing away a boo-boo.

I suck in a breath, shocked by the tender display.

Slowly, his head lifts. "We'd make quite the pair, snowflake. But I'm too hard for your soft."

My breath catches again. He isn't talking about body parts. He's talking about him.

"I need to make a phone call." The abrupt change in his demeanor leaves me speechless as he excuses himself.

Holding a paper towel around my finger, I remain in the kitchen wondering what he meant.

Who made you hard, fireman?
And what would it take to soften him?

day 2

two turtles and dovetails

December 27

chapter 5

[Brock]

Dinner last night was both strained and silent. I couldn't seem to pull my eyes away from her. I hated what I heard her say about herself. Even worse was that she thought I was calling her names. I might be a mean bastard, but I'd never do that.

She was fucking beautiful with that dark hair in contrast to her white clothing. I wanted to see that dark hair spread out on an ivory pillow and the rest of her pale skin on display, but I wasn't allowing myself the vision. Not after admitting how I'd like to feel her beneath my hands.

We could never be a couple. Which was too bad because I missed coupling. Not just the sex but the companionship. The one plus one equals one. The soft to my hard.

Rolling my head on the bed pillow, I stare at a picture on Cap's nightstand. When Pear first brought me to his bedroom, I felt a little strange taking his bed. However, I either slept here or on the sofa, and while that living room furniture looked comfy, it also appeared a little too well-loved for my aging back.

The image of two girls, roughly six- or seven-years old, smiling with a matching set of missing front teeth stares back at me. Each girl has some kind of circular chest shield on their front. One has a scarf around her eyes with slits for the eye holes. The other has a scarf pushed back on her head like a headband.

Are they dressed like *Teenage Mutant Ninja Turtles*?

I'm reminded of my own kids at such a young age. I worked a lot back then. Two days on. One day off. Still, I made the time to be involved with Nick and Ellie. Taking on lunch duty at the school when parent-volunteers were needed. Helping coach Little League baseball and Pop Warner football for Nick. I attended all of Ellie's dance recitals and Girl Scout stuff. Sometimes I'd be the only dad in the audience for her things.

My active attendance was a result of my own father's absence. Deciding one day he didn't want a family anymore, he left Ma, me, my younger brother, Zebb, and my little sister, Marnie, to fend for ourselves. People like to say Zebb took on the responsibility of caring for the family. He got a scholarship to the fancy college, played in the NFL, and made the big bucks. He came home a hero as a single dad to the most amazing little girl.

However, I'd gone directly into the CFD upon graduating high school because we couldn't afford to send an average kid to college. Scholarships didn't knock on the door of a star athlete with mediocre grades. And I couldn't leave Ma alone with Zebb and Marnie. Someone had to stay behind and take care of the old house, plus help with my siblings.

I'd done that.

So, I let off steam once in a while. Caused a little trouble here and there. Was too loud.

My heart has always been in the right place. For Ma. For Zebb and Marnie, too. Their lives hadn't been any easier than mine in some ways, but I still tried to ease their paths.

As for my kids, I showed up day and night, even when Melissa and I started to fight. When she wanted more, and we didn't have the means. She took a job and started contributing to the household funds, but also spent more than we made collectively. I didn't want to deny my wife nice things, but we couldn't always purchase the most expensive items either. I wasn't a miser; but I wasn't a millionaire.

We bought a house that needed work, and I fixed it up which took time, effort, and patience.

We sent our kids to the fancy private school, valuing the education and dismissing the cost, but it didn't entitle Nick to get a Jeep at sixteen or allow Ellie to own some fancy-schmancy purse and shoes like the other girls.

My kids didn't complain. Melissa did.

Instead, I tried to *be present* for my kids. I wanted them to understand working hard and being an honest person paid off, but had I told them often enough how proud I was of them? How Nick was my hero for sticking his ground and sticking up for the underdog at times. Or telling Ellie she wasn't just the apple of my eye but everything I'd hoped would come to fruition in a daughter of mine. Strong, independent, a smart young woman. Beautiful, both inside and out.

For some reason, canning pears brought it all back to me. Working hard at something simple helped me remember that not everything needed to be bought from a store. Sure, it was easier at times. Maybe even cheaper in some cases. But there was a real sense of accomplishment in creating something from scratch.

I might have made a huge mess in Cap's kitchen and accepted Pear's offer to help clean it all up, especially with my hand still stinging, but dammit, it felt good to be productive.

Even if it was Valentine's Day pears.

Never heard of Valentine pears but I'll be telling all my friends they need them for their wives and girlfriends.

What said love better than a pear.

+ + +

Slipping into the kitchen, the open concept space is chilly this morning without a blazing fire in the fireplace. Cap's bedroom had been cool last night but nestled beneath layers of blankets and a thick comforter, I was almost too hot in the middle of the night. I'd slept better than I'd slept in months, maybe years, and I couldn't explain it because I didn't like to sleep anywhere but in my own bed.

To my surprise, a bright red mug sits beside the coffee maker which happens to be ON. *She didn't know how to use the machine, my ass.*

A note is propped up against a cannister. "Meet me in Dad's workshop. Second building. Behind the barn."

A quick glance out the window shows the snow piled up overnight, but a path is formed from the house to the barn.

I don't like that Paradise has already been up and shoveling snow while I lingered in her dad's bed staring at a photo of two kids. Assuming the image is Pear and her sister, I don't recall Cap speaking often about his girls.

Have I not been listening? Have I been that negligent as a co-worker and friend? How did I not know he not only had one daughter but two? Cap lost his wife a long time ago and never remarried.

What was it he said to the guys?

"When you find the one woman that makes you glow inside, every other woman pales in comparison."

Shaking my head, I chuckle. Never considered Cap romantic.

I glance down at my waiting mug and the coffee dripping into the maker. When was the last time someone had done something that showed they cared about me? I almost laugh at the thought. Then I reconsider. When was the last time I'd done something thoughtful for someone else? And I'm not thinking of Ma or Marnie. But for a woman.

Staring at the coffee maker filling with liquid gold, I search for an answer and come up empty. My chest squeezes at the void.

Pear called me crass yesterday, then a dick. I shouldn't care what she thinks of me, but I do. I don't need her to like me, but I don't want her to think poorly of me either.

It shouldn't matter.

But it does.

+ + +

I wasn't surprised to find Pear, as I was planning to call her, in white snow bibs and a white sweatshirt. The ivory-colored knit cap was on her head again, but her hands were busy sanding a spindle-backed bench. Hunched over with her ass in the air, her back is to me as I enter.

"What is all this?" I chuckle, glancing around at the collection of tools, a work bench, and several pieces of furniture in various states of disrepair. A cast-iron, wood-burning stove stands in a corner taking the chill out of the air, but not actually heating the space of this single-story structure that appeared as rundown on the outside as the barn. However, it's rather cozy inside this space.

Pear lifts her head, her eyes wide. "You really need to come with a warning."

As she focuses on me, my face heats and I arch a brow. Good to know she finds me attractive. "Oh really?"

"Yeah, a nice set of sleigh bells to let someone know you're approaching." She stands upright and faces me.

"Oh." I scoff. *Not attracted to me*. Got it. "Anyway . . . what's all this?"

"Day two for you." She giggles at her own rhyme. "Dad mentioned you are good at wood working."

Is she questioning my ability? And did she say her dad has mentioned me? Who knows what Cap has told Pear about me. Probably the truth. Which worries me more than it should.

She continues, "So he has this dresser." She points toward a low, three-drawer dresser painted white.

"And that child's cabinet." She nods toward a mid-chest-high piece of furniture with one long drawer at the top and several smaller ones stacked on top of each other next to a low door. The piece is rather unique.

"A few of the dovetail joints are missing." Pear steps closer to the first dresser. "In fact, the front panel for this one is broken, and I'm hoping you can repair it."

I stare at Pear a long moment before stepping closer to the furniture and inspecting the structure. Dovetailing is a traditional way to build furniture and cabinets, and a craft that went out of style for a while, then returned to fashion. With pressed wood being the major component of most modern furniture, it's rare to find dovetail work in pieces unless the item has been hand-crafted or is an antique. This set of dressers falls into both categories.

"I'd need glue and a hand chisel, and—" I stop as Pear opens her arm to wave around us.

"Everything you need should be here and if it's not, you'll need to make do. Dad's words. Not mine." Pear shakes her head like she's exasperated by her father or maybe she's just sick of playing messenger.

"Maybe you should just give me the list of things Cap wants done and I'll check them off as I go."

"No can do, fireman. Dad says—" She cuts herself short when I start to scoff.

I've lost count on how many times she says *Dad says*. "Look, just give me the list."

"No." Her firm tone is accentuated when she places her hands on her hips. "You'll get a project every day and—"

"If you give me the list, I can speed things up. Maybe cut out two birds with one stone, maybe even three in a day."

"I don't want you taking out two birds. You have twelve days to fulfill."

"Aw, snowflake, are you trying to keep me here?" I chide. "That's sweet."

"You wish." She rolls her eyes and returns to sanding the bench. Her delicate hand wraps around a spindle, and she works it up and down, up and down, rubbing at the cylinder piece in sharp, quick jerks to strip it clean.

My thoughts run rampant.

Jesus. I rub a hand down my face, feeling the scratch of my scruff. I need to get a grip on myself and the internal innuendo. Visions of her stroking me that way, giving me a release, have no place here.

Removing my jacket as the space is warm enough and working will only further heat me, I look through Cap's tools and find an old hand chisel. What I really need is a dovetail saw . . . *and oh my God*, Cap has one, plus a square level and beveled angle level. Cap's work bench is a woodworker's dream.

"I didn't know Cap was into woodworking or building furniture."

"Oh, he's not. This stuff was left over from when Dad bought the place. The former owner was a cabinet maker or something like that."

Admiring the tools I'll use, I run my fingertips over the edges. The sharp angles. The dulled points.

"You okay?" Pear asks.

"It's nothing." I step over to the dresser first, examining what needs to be done. The piece of furniture is small and white, which leads me to believe it belonged to a child at one time.

"Tell me," she prompts.

"It's stu—" I glance up at her, catching her eyes and watching her brows sternly press together, daring me to say the word. As much as I want her to playfully scold me like the bad boy I can be, this is different.

"I'd love to build furniture."

"Really?" Those pinched brows hitch higher, surprise and curiosity filling her blue eyes.

"Yes, really." Is it so hard to believe? "My ex didn't believe I could. She wanted . . . well, it doesn't matter."

Pear is quiet a moment, but I can feel her eyes on me as I crouch down to further inspect the busted drawer.

"I have an ex, too."

I freeze before slowly standing. "Who the fuck would leave you?"

Those raised brows morph into a startled expression. "Actually, I left him."

"Of course you did."

"What's that supposed to mean?" With her hip cocked, she places one fist on it and glares at me, those blue eyes icy.

"It means no man in his fucking right mind would leave you. You had to have left him. What he'd do? Take all your money? Fuck your best friend? Leave you with the kids?"

With my mouth running, I hardly notice Pear lower her head, eyes drifting to the cement floor at our feet.

"You don't deserve that story, either." She turns back to the bench she's working on, her hand moving faster over the spindle. Her attention aggressive and hyper-focused.

Fuck! I turn back toward the broken dresser but pause, staring blindly down at the open drawer and the tools I spread on the top surface.

"I'm sorry," I mutter.

The distinct sound of sandpapering continues.

"I said, I'm sorry," I say louder and turn to face Pear.

She stills but doesn't remove her hand from the spindle or draw her eyes away from the bench.

"That's what happened to me. My story. She broke us financially. Then fucked my best friend in our bed. Left me and the kids for Kenny. Fucking Kenny." I turn back toward the dresser and place both my hands on the top. Spreading my arms, I lean on the piece as if I need support. "I'm over it. But sometimes, it still stings."

I pause. "She wanted more than I could give her, but even if I gave her everything, I don't think she'd ever have been happy." Quietly, I add, "With me."

Silence filters between us. I close my eyes. Fucking Kenny. Sometimes it hurt more that I'd lost my best friend than my wife.

"He said I was getting fat."

I spin so fast my hip hits the dresser and it wobbles. With a firm hand slapping the top, the furniture stills, but I keep my hand on the surface, bracing myself once more.

"He said what?" I see fire. Flames are certain to be flashing in my eyes. Smoke steaming out my ears.

Pear glances away from me, gaze fixated on something across the room. "I'd married him during a vulnerable time in my life."

She shrugs and peers back at me. "My worth isn't measured by my dress size, but *he* was no longer happy with me. How I looked. How I dressed. None of that mattered, though, compared to how he used me, lied to me, much like your ex-wife. He had a gambling problem. Put up our house as collateral without telling me. Loans and liens on almost everything we'd owned. We owed three years' worth of back taxes. It was a financial shitshow."

Her eyes turn cloudy. "He was interested in staying married, only he was no longer interested in me." Rapidly blinking away the storm, she adds. "And I didn't want or need what he offered. I'm worth more than that."

"Damn right you are."

With our eyes locked on one another, my body vibrates with anger. The desire to close the distance between us and pull her to my chest is powerfully strong. I want to draw her close to me, and yet, at the same time, I'm afraid. Afraid she'll break me. Afraid I'll break her.

"We're quite a pair," I softly remark.

"A pair," she whispers.

When I can no longer take the intensity of those blue eyes staring at me, I turn back to the dresser, and at first, mindlessly begin working on repairing the dovetail joints. The soft sound of sandpaper schussing over wood fills my ears, giving me strange comfort. Working to repair the dresser actually brings me joy.

Pear and I seem to have come to an understanding.

Sometimes quiet moments matter more.

+ + +

I not only finished working on both dressers, but asked if there was anything else I could do.

Pear's gaze fixates on the child's pieces for a long moment before stating, "I'm not certain why Dad saved the white one. It belonged to my sister. As for the child's chest, I think he was just putzing with that one. Maybe planning to resell it."

"Is that the plan for the bench?"

Pear turns her gaze back to the bench which has had a thorough sanding and looks ready to be stained or painted. A soft smile curls her lips. "The bench was my mother's. From our old house back in Chicago. Dad could never part with it after Mom—" Pear shakes her head, unable to speak.

Cap's wife was Pear's mom. How had I not put two and two together?

"When did she pass?"

"I was eleven."

"My dad left when I was ten. Not quite the same thing, but I know Cap never remarried and neither did my ma." Another understanding. We were both raised by single parents.

Her tender smile doesn't change but her eyes shift. Compassion and further understanding fills them. Perhaps a little girl needed her mother growing up. I certainly wish my dad had been present.

Waving a hand in the air, like I'm swatting at dust, I say, "But enough sad stories for one day, yeah?"

"Yeah." Her voice remains quiet as she turns back to the bench but slowly stands. Her hands press at her lower back, and she arches backward. "I don't think my body is made to squat like that for so long. I'm not as flexible as I used to be."

Lifting my hand to my mouth, I bite my knuckles. Images of her in a variety of positions race through my head. On her back. On her knees. I don't need her to be flexible. I just want to be close to her. But we've already established there's a thin line between us. One called her dad, and the other called my penance. I'm not here to mess anything up.

Still, I can't help the visions dancing in my head of her and me, and an overstuffed bed.

"Get your mind out of the gutter, fireman," she calls, giving me a knowing smirk.

I chuckle. "How'd you know it was in the gutter?"

"You have a certain gleam in your eye when your thoughts drop below my belt."

"Oh yeah. Been checking out my eyes, have you?"

"Been looking below my belt?"

I won't deny it, but I also won't admit that I have trouble peeling my gaze from those hips. Or her ass. My fingers itch to dig into that firm flesh and just squeeze.

Something flies through the air, gaining my attention, but dropping before my boot-covered toes. Glancing downward, I find the sandpaper she'd been using balled up and inches from my foot.

"Did you just try to throw something at me?"

She shrugs, but her teeth dig into the corner of her lower lip.

"If you're gonna toss something—"

"Don't you dare say I throw like a girl. Like that would be an insult." Her cocky confidence has my body humming in a new way.

"I was going to say, at least make it something that can go the distance."

"Yeah?" She chews harder at her mouth before her eyes shift toward the door.

The energy around us spikes. It's been a good day. I feel accomplished working on the furniture. I also feel a little lighter sharing about Melissa. The circumstance of my marriage is a familiar tale with the guys in the firehouse. However, the situation isn't something I easily share with others, especially women. Telling Pear felt right and hearing her story felt good, too.

When her eyes shift left again, I follow her gaze. "What are you looking at?"

She lifts her index finger and taps at her lower lip, drawing my attention to the cherry-red plumpness. "Thinking about what I could throw at you . . . that would go the distance."

Her heart? The thought is foolish.

"And it's something over there?" I nod toward the closed work shed door where her eyes shift. A variety of tools are off to the right on a bench. However, I don't think she's looking to clobber me over the head with a hammer.

"Not exactly."

"Something outside?" I question, slowly registering what she might be thinking as I step closer to her. "You wouldn't?"

"A little snow might be a good way to cool you off, fireman."

"Admit it, you have the hots for me, snowflake."

"Oh, I have something for you, alright."

With that taunt, she's racing for the door. I drop the tools I'm holding, quick to chase her. With a hard push on the workshop door, the barrier swings open and a blast of snowy air hits us. Pear high-foot steps along the trail she shoveled earlier. In the warmth of the brilliant afternoon sunshine, the path she made has melted into a pebble and ice strip. However, she isn't running for the house. She stops short near a pile of snow and cups a handful of the icy mixture.

"You're looking at the snowball champion of Chicago, snowflake," I warn her as I dip my hands into the snowy drift near me and masterfully form a solid ball. Before I'm finished, something hard and wet pelts my shoulder.

Pear's mouth falls open when I look at her. Then her hands fist on her hips. "Well, you're looking at the snowball champion of Paradise Farms." Her arms spread wide, just begging for me to peg her with the snowball in my hand.

I have a better idea. In three long strides, I'm in her space. When she registers how close I am, she turns to run, but I'm quick to catch her by the cross-back of her snow bibs and tug her to my chest. She removed her knit cap at some point and pulled her hair into a long ponytail, high on the back of her head. With the icy ball packed in my hand, I rub it against the side of her neck to her nape.

"That's so cold," she squeals, delight mixing with irritation.

"You said my fire needs some ice."

"I didn't say—" Her breath hitches because my warm mouth is sucking at the icy mess melting against her skin and sliding down the back of her neck.

My teeth drag against the column of her throat in a playful squeeze. My lips close around her cold flesh, and I suck.

"*Fuuudge*," she whispers, low and seductive, while bending forward which brings her backside against my front. Layers prevent us from meeting properly but the wedge in my pants rivals the strength of any tool in the workshop. I'm hard as steel.

With an arm around her waist, and my mouth suctioned to her skin, I travel over her neck, scraping and licking, rolling my tongue against her chilled flesh. I wrap her ponytail around my fist and tug her head back so I can get to the front of her throat. My hand cups her jaw, tilting her head even more. She gasps again.

My lips track her hard swallow, and I drag my teeth over the edge of her chin. My mouth is almost to hers.

Breathlessly, she whispers, "We shouldn't do this."

I freeze. Teeth on her chin. Lips eager to close the millimeters between our mouths. Her words weren't coldly stated. Actually, the heat of her breath tickles my nose. But she's right.

What am I doing?

Quickly, I stand upright and release her. Running my icy hand down my face, I close my eyes a second before turning my head away from her. Then I bring my attention back to her. Her blue eyes are dilated and wide. Her breath comes short and quick.

"Fuck. I'm sorry. I'm not here to take advantage of you."

"I know."

"That was . . ." Uncalled for. Unexpected. Unbelievably fucking hot.

She's already shaking her head, dismissing anything I might say. "It's okay. I teased you to chase." She pats my chest, patronizing and pathetic, as if I'm a silly child. Then, she circles around me and heads back to the workshop while I stand in the cold air, staring up a crystal blue sky that mirrors Pear's eyes.

Cursing myself, I realize under different circumstances, I'd like the chance to chase her.

No teasing necessary.

chapter 6

[Pear]

That kiss was so hot, it melted snow. Literally. Bits and pieces had trickled down my back and no amount of cooling could tamp down the heat rushing through my body.

While I cleaned up today's progress on the bench, Brock returned to the work shed and sheepishly asked if he could use a small chunk of wood he found for something. I shrugged but nodded. We worked in comfortable silence for a while longer, even as the air around us sizzled. I was aware of every noise and movement Brock made, even though I kept my head down, pretending as if that kiss hadn't just thawed an inch of the ice surrounding my heart.

When we finally exited the workshop together and I locked the door, Brock immediately offered to go to the grocery store. Sensing we needed some space after that near-kiss and heated attack on my neck, I let him go.

Strangely, I worry he won't come back. This was his out. Not that I was holding him prisoner, but he could drive off and decide not to return. Dad isn't here to demand Brock focus, and Brock made it clear he'd rather not be here at all.

However, yesterday, he gave pear canning a valiant effort, and today he worked diligently on the set of dressers. Keeping his hands busy might have helped clear his mind. That had been my hope for myself when I started sanding Mom's old bench. The piece would look perfect here on the front porch of the farmhouse. If this place was my parents' dream, Dad should have the bench on display, not buried in his work shed with other random antiques. Mom's favorite piece was meant to be enjoyed and used, not hidden.

That had been Dad's explanation for the holiday decorations that draped and dripped throughout his house. My mom loved Christmas and their treasured ornaments and traditions should be brought into the light once a year. My dad was rather sentimental. Which also might have explained why he still had the white dresser that belonged to my sister as a child. He had trouble letting go of objects that held memories.

As for me, I often believed it was better to remove an item than to stare it in the face. An object was only an object. It didn't hold value, at least not mentally.

Seeing my mom's bench had me second guessing my old opinion. However, I didn't take the time to delve any deeper into my thoughts, as I had bigger issues.

Personal business to attend to. Namely, relieving the ache Brock had produced with his opened-mouth suction on my neck. The way he held my jaw, positioned between his thumb and forefinger. So dominating. So tantalizing. And then those teeth.

While I stand beneath the spray of a warm shower, I shiver. My skin was chilled from the contrast of the sweat I'd worked up all morning and the snow that melted down my back. But as my body turns pink underneath the heated water, my thoughts turn red hot. Tickling my fingers between my breasts, it feels wrong to be turned on by Brock. Wrong to take care of myself without him present, but isn't that what men do all the time? A little relief in the shower to clear their heads; pun intended.

As my fingers linger at my waist, drawing circles around my belly button, I smile to myself, recalling Brock's angry reaction to my comment yesterday about being *the fat girl* and my admission today about Reggie and his repulsion over the changes in my body. I've always been a solid girl. Broad shoulders, wide hips. My stomach was flatter when I was younger. My breasts smaller, too. Each decade seems to add ten pounds, though, and I went through a period where I didn't try to fight the weight gain.

I typically live life with an equal balance between healthy diet and regular exercise, but I'm not going to deny myself good food or a little fun on occasion. What can I say? I like to eat.

I close my eyes and cleanse myself of the negative reminders of my past. My fingers travel lower, and I envision Brock on his knees before me. That mouth of his, warm and wet, sucking on the sensitive nub currently pulsing with need. Those teeth scraping over tender folds, drawing out the building tension. Then that tongue . . . *hmm*, his tongue. Long and thick, hot and hungry, would work with teasing aggression like he did against my neck as he devours me.

I shiver once more, but this time with pleasure. As my fingers stroke between my legs, my mouth falls open in a silent gasp. My eyes remain closed, while tiny snowflakes flicker behind my lids and a rush of heat warms my lower belly, sparks flaring against an area that's been cold for too long.

Brock's name is a silent whisper in my head as I come hot and fast.

I'm not one to have one-night stands, and I hadn't been on many dates that lead to more than kissing. My focus has been elsewhere over the past three years, but now . . . *this* is why I'd come to Paradise Farms.

I wanted a new direction for my stagnant life.

And Brock Scroggs had ignited something else that has been dormant.

My libido is back.

+ + +

When Brock hadn't returned once I exited the shower and dressed, thoughts of him abandoning his twelve days, now down to almost ten, flit through my head again. Attempting to calm my galloping mind, I start a small fire and curl into the red plaid chair in the corner. I love this spot for reflection and if the Christmas tree wasn't present, I'd be able to stare out the window from this position.

With another mug of hot chocolate, splashed with a hint of peppermint, minus the alcohol, I ponder my life choices. Decisions I've made. Conversations I've had. Things that are all so meaningless as I can't change the past. And wishing I could go back is like shoveling during a snowstorm. Not going to get me anywhere but cold and exhausted.

Through therapy, I've been able to release the mistake of marrying Reggie. Forgive myself for the things I hadn't seen in our marriage. Forgive him for the doubts he placed in me about myself. If nothing else, the past three years have taught me how much of a survivor I am.

I'd stayed in a job I never really loved to work off the debt that Reggie had incurred in our name.

I'd divorced him and sought the help I needed for the mental damage caused in our marriage.

I'd come to terms with tragic personal loss.

What I hadn't done, though, was tell my dad everything. He'd willingly have given up anything to help me, but I didn't want that. I hadn't wanted to lay my burdens on him. He'd had enough in his lifetime. I didn't want to be the cause of more stress. Plus, I was a grown adult. I'd made my decisions, which turned out to be mistakes, and I had to forgive myself for being human.

I'd fallen. I'd risen back up. In between those two points had been the rough patch.

This didn't mean I didn't still have some emotional scars. My issues weren't abandonment but loss. I'd lost my mother when I was young. I'd lost my way when I married Reggie. I'd lost—

The front door swings open and a blast of cold air whirls into the room, cutting off my rambling thoughts. I stand instantly.

Brock enters, weighed down by plastic grocery bags dangling off each of his wrists. With his booted foot, he nudges the door closed with his heel, and stumbles forward.

"You came back." A question lingers in the declaration. He wasn't gone that long, honestly.

Still, my heart is racing, and I place my hand over my chest as if the movement can calm the rapid pattering. Maybe I was more worried than

I thought that Brock wouldn't return. That he'd drive off to Chicago without a word, and I'd never see him again.

The sound of cans and boxes lightly thud on the wooden dining table as Brock struggles to release his wrists from the plentiful sacks.

"What is all this?" I chuckle, attempting to clear the evident surprise and slight relief from my throat as I step closer to the table.

"Explain that reaction." His rugged voice, growly and demanding, has me lifting my head and meeting his dark eyes.

"What reaction?"

"Why wouldn't I come back?" His head tilts to the side, and those coal-colored eyes flicker with a tiny speck of light. A diamond hidden in the rough.

I shrug, gazing down at the collection of bags spread across the table. Reaching for one, I toy with the handle to avoid the pressure of him watching me.

"Snowflake?" he encourages.

"I just thought you might want to escape. Heading to the store would be your chance to ditch this gig." Sheepishly, I glance up to find his eyes wide and mouth agape.

"I am not a quitter." He'd vehemently said the same thing yesterday but this time his tone is tender, cautious.

"I know, but I still thought . . ."

"I'd never leave without saying goodbye." His penetrating eyes are still watching me, and I glance down at the grocery bags again. In less than twelve days, goodbye might be the only thing he'll say to me.

"It's not that."

"Then what *is* it?"

How do I explain myself? Was I worried that I'd lose him, too? That was ridiculous. I'd only met him yesterday. So what if he sucked at my neck today in a way I'd never been kissed before. We weren't life partners. We weren't soulmates. We weren't the pair he kept calling us.

"Nothing," I state as I reach for a bag in the middle of the table that toppled over from its own weight.

Brock catches my wrist, causing me to look up at him. His tender squeeze demands I answer.

"I just thought you'd leave."

His mouth quirks, the corner rising. "I'd think you'd be happy to see me go."

"It isn't awful spending time with you, I guess."

His smile spreads wider, salacious, sensual. How had I not noticed his mouth before? Those lush lips. The white teeth sneaking out with his grin. And don't forget that silvery scruff on his jaw growing thicker by the hour.

"Yeah. You aren't awful either." He winks, and I'm like a match lighting on the first strike. My insides blaze and my cheeks warm, but the molten desire between my legs hits the hardest. I want to swipe the groceries off this table and climb over it on my hands and knees, tug at the collar of his jacket and pull him to me, where I'd crush my mouth against his and—

"Pear?"

Oh my God. Did I say any of that fantasy aloud? I take a second to consciously review the last few minutes, worrying that my vivid imaginings came out in a verbal seduction. The quick check tells me I've kept my thoughts to myself, and I tug at my arm so Brock will release my wrist.

"I'm good."

He hums as his eyes roam from my hair to my stomach and back to my eyes.

"So what did you buy?" I ask as a way of distraction.

"My woman wanted roast beast, so I bought us one." He rustles through the plastic bags and removes a beef tenderloin that's big enough to feed twelve, not two.

My breath catches from what he'd said. *His woman.* I could run a whole commentary on why calling me his woman is inappropriate and misogynist, but I'm stuck on another set of words. Roast beast. He caught the reference yesterday. And the little grinch before me shifts from a green heathen to a too-cute, fuzzy-soft creature.

"Aw, fireman, don't make me like you."

"I'm hard to resist." His grin shifts to a knowing smirk.

Yeah, he knows he's hot, but he isn't looking at me cocky and confident. He's staring at me like a hungry man, fighting off his desires while desperate to satisfy them.

"I also got you these." From another bag, he removes a bouquet of hothouse-grown white tulips. The flower is so out of season and yet surprisingly refreshing.

"Are these apology flowers?" Is he sorry he kissed me earlier?

He shrugs. "Hadn't really considered that." He lifts his hand and scratches underneath his chin with his knuckles. The raspy sound does nothing to chill the gooey warmth in my lower belly.

"Just saw them and thought of you, snowflake."

My face heats, suddenly realizing these aren't simply last-second I'm sorry, flowers. That warmth down low becomes molten lava. Emotions that I should suppress can't be wrangled. Brock wants to feed me. He bought me flowers because he thought of me. I almost don't know what to do with this unexpected kindness.

"That was sweet."

Reaching into his pants pocket, he pulls out something else. He holds out his cupped hand and inside is something made of wood.

"It's a snowflake." I lift my head, shock in my voice. "Did you make that? For me?"

He shrugs. "Just playing around." His voice lowers, vulnerable and hesitant. I can almost hear his thoughts telling him it's nothing. It's stupid. But before he can retract his gift, an object I'll treasure forever, I take it from him and press it to my chest.

His thoughtfulness will be my unraveling.

"That's my apology."

He has nothing to be sorry about. I'd take a thousand hot kisses from him, and every wooden snowflake he wants to make me.

+ + +

We don't eat the beef. Instead, Brock bought a still-steaming, rotisserie chicken that comes with two sides and cornbread. We never had lunch and he admitted he was starving, so he wanted something hot and quick once he returned.

We ate in relative silence again. Brock rushing to eat. Me savoring the food.

After our lunch-slash-dinner, Brock showers and I return to the chair in the corner until he re-enters the living room and asks me if I want a glass of wine. I stand and meet him in the kitchen.

"Is this allowed on the job?" He holds up a brown bottle of beer for himself.

"I won't tell, if you don't." I have no idea if Dad allows his restorative group to drink alcohol while on retreat. I'd guess yes, but if someone's issue was with drugs or alcohol, I'd suspect no.

"Why did Dad want you on his retreat?"

Brock pops the cap on his beer and picks up the glass of wine he poured for me, nodding toward the couch for us to sit.

He follows me to the broken-in cushions and hands me the glass of red. We each take a corner of the couch. I lean my side into the back cushions and prop my arm on it, holding up my head as I face Brock. He slouches into the lumpy cushions and stares at the fire dancing in the hearth. He rests the open beer bottle at his waistline. He's wearing black joggers and a long-sleeved waffle-weave shirt with three buttons open at the neck. Why is it loungewear can look so sexy on a man?

"I hit someone."

My arm drops and I sit upright. Brock turns only his head to look at me. "We'd been drinking, shooting the shit, when Dane mentioned Melissa, my ex." Brock looks away again, lifts his beer and takes a long drink. "He made some wisecrack about Melissa fucking Kenny. Some quip I can't even recall now, but I snapped. Clocked him right in the nose."

Brock makes a fist and imitates a rather weak punch. When his hand settles back around his beer bottle, he sighs. "I overreacted. Always do." Sarcasm fills his voice.

"Why?"

"Why what?" He glances at me again.

"Why did you react with your fist?"

"What are you? My shrink?" His voice is rough, like the gravel in the drive and reminiscent of the man who arrived two mornings ago.

"Do you need one?"

"No." He scoffs.

"I did."

Brock stares at me and if attending therapy just changed his mind about me, if he even had an opinion of me, we cannot be friends. He might be hot on the outside, but I can't deal with shallow on the inside again.

His eyelids lower and he swallows hard. "Why did you need a shrink?"

"I didn't need a shrink. I needed help growing taller." I sit even straighter. "I'd been brought down but I wanted to stand up again."

Brock's gaze lifts to my face. "What happened?"

I shake my head. "Gotta earn my stories, fireman." And his attitude about therapy has just knocked him over to the naughty list, and not the playfully naughty one.

A tiny smirk curls his mouth. "And how do I earn a snowflake story?"

"Tell me one of your own."

He remains silent a moment. Maybe he needs a nudge, maybe a prompt, to get him talking.

"Are you still in love with Melissa? Is that why you reacted?"

"No." The rejection is punctuated by a bitter laugh.

"But it still stings that she stepped out on you?"

"She didn't step out. She fucked someone in *our* bed."

"And not just someone, but your best friend." I pause. "I can see how that would hurt. Blur those marriage vows a bit," I tease. I'm not mocking his pain, but I want to lessen the tension. "And cross the bro-code line."

"Yeah. Bro-code." Again, his voice is full of bitter mockery.

"When did the divorce happen?"

"Nick was in high school. Ellie in eighth grade." He pauses, thinking. "The most shocking part was who she was with."

After a moment, he sighs. "Kenny was my best friend. We started in the department together. And as my best friend, I went to Kenny with my worries and concerns. About how stressed I was over Melissa and her spending habits. Her attitude about money. And then she fucked her. And now they're getting married."

"Wait. What? *She* and *her*."

"Kennedy is a woman."

Oh my. "Love is love," I whisper.

"Well, I didn't want my best friend loving my wife. Or marrying her."

Totally understandable. "So, when is the big day?"

Brock brings his beer to his mouth again, takes a long pull, and swallows hard. There's a *bop* sound as his lips release the bottle. "This week."

Double oh my.

"My kids are with them. They're having a destination wedding. In Wisconsin."

This makes me laugh. I like Wisconsin well enough but it's not exactly the place I'd consider a destination for a wedding.

"Some fancy hotel in the northern part. A real winter wonderland for their wedding."

"Is the expensive, exclusive wedding the issue or the marriage?"

"Does it matter?" He runs his thumb nail over the bottle's label.

"You don't want her marrying someone else?"

"I don't want to be unmarried myself," he finally states, loud and agitated.

My eyes widen at this response. "Are you saying you miss being married?"

Brock lifts his beer bottle again, and drinks heartily. His Adam's apple bobs as he swallows gulp after gulp. When he finishes, he stares down at the empty container and shrugs.

"I liked being married. Liked knowing that at the end of the day, Melissa and I were coming home to each other. We were partners. We were together. Or at least, we had been at first." He exhales. "I always wanted a family. A unit that was my own. I have a nice house and great kids. And at least, my kids were happy to see me." He sighs. "Eventually, I'm not certain they were so thrilled."

"What happened with your kids?"

Brock shakes his head, darkness suddenly marring his features. This is a subject he won't touch. We've already crossed a line speaking about his ex-wife.

However, his admission about marriage is reassuring. I'd have never guessed Brock might have a little romantic nature buried deep inside him.

That path is dangerous. I don't need to get ahead of myself. That's how I ended up with Reggie.

"What about you? You were married. Don't you miss it?"

"I don't miss him, that's for sure." I chuckle, more good-natured than Brock about my ex. Our marriage didn't fall apart with a human third party involved. Gambling was Reggie's mistress, and while no less deceitful, at least it wasn't a physical person, or my best friend, that made him unfaithful.

Unfortunately, I can't tell Brock what I really miss, whether in marriage or otherwise. *Sex.* Rather than a true love bringing me a bird in a fruit tree, he should bring on the orgasms.

Brock snorts, drawing my attention back to him. "Guess we aren't meant for true love."

My brows pinch. "Oh, I still believe in true love."

Brock leans forward, bracing his elbows on his legs while turning his head to look at me again. "Even after your marriage failed?"

"I didn't fail at loving. Had I once thought I loved Reggie? I did. Evidently not true love, but love in all its mysterious, foggy ways. And I still believe true love is out there." I dramatically wave through the air. "Somewhere."

Silence falls between us a second before I add, "My parents had a true-love match."

With a pensive hum, Brock lowers his head to peer at the fire. The blaze is dying back and his gaze lifts higher to the decorative panels above the mantel. He tips his beer bottle toward the bird images painted on the doors.

"Doves. Mates for life."

"My mother loved the birds," I state, my voice low at the sudden reminder of my mom. A misty haze of memory where she is laughing and my dad cups her face, bringing her close for a kiss. He was so sweet on her.

Clearing my throat, I nod toward the panels. "But those birds don't mean romantic love. They represent . . ." My throat grows thicker. "They represent my sister and me. Pear." I point at the left panel. "And Peach. My twin sister."

"Ah, the ninja turtles in the photo on Cap's bedside table."

Dad still has that picture? I hadn't noticed. It's been years since I've been here, seeing Dad more often in Chicago. Yesterday, I only changed the sheets on the bed and did a quick scan of the room for dirty laundry. I didn't give the framed images on his bedside table a second glance.

Softly, I smile. "My sister loved turtles and begged me to dress up as one for Halloween to match her. Our mom was still alive then and our parents joined in. The four of us represented *The Teenage Mutant Ninja Turtles*." Melancholy hits like a blunt sword.

Brock lightly chuckles, as if he can picture the four of us. Then again, he saw how Peach and I looked in our costumes.

"Pear and Peach, cute."

"Paradise and Precious. Our mother wanted to be original. Wanted us to stand out."

My gaze is focused on the panels. I can't remember exactly when we painted them. Dad cut the squared doors. Peach and I fought over which color should represent us. She wanted green. I wanted hot pink.

Dad settled the argument by having her use muted blue and me a dusty rose.

"Mom always said we were two halves of one soul. Her little birds." Giving us such different names and then slicing those names even further into fruit endearments made no sense. But Dad called Mom a mother hen and we were her chicks. The loves of her life.

Marriage. Motherhood. Sisters. So many ways to love. So many versions of soulmates.

"Cap doesn't really talk about you or your sister." Brock speaks softly, quietly sharing the information I'm well aware of. When Peach and I were younger, he'd tell us he wanted to protect us. Fireman and cop kids could be targets. When we grew older, Peach thought the distance he put between his teenage daughters and the firehouse was to keep probies away from us. Or us away from the new recruits. Fiery hot fireman and hormonal girls can be a flammable combination.

"It's hard for him. My mom. And my sister."

Brock's eyes remain on me, but I lower my gaze from the painted panels to stare at my lap.

"Christmas can be the loneliest time of the year." I swallow, willing away the prickle in my nose and burn in my dry eyes. A sharp crack goes off in the fireplace, and I close my eyes willing away the constant ache. This isn't where I wanted our conversation to veer.

"Peach was only twenty-eight. I should have felt her sadness. If we shared a soul like we shared the womb, I should have known something was wrong. But I didn't."

I look back at the painted panels, blinking harder to clear the mist in my eyes. Every day I ache for her as my other half. I tried to fit Reggie into the void, but he'd only taken advantage of my vulnerability. Plus, sisterly love was different than marriage. No one can ever patch the gap her senseless, unexpected death left in my heart.

"Snowflake," Brock mumbles, setting his empty beer bottle at his feet and sliding closer to me on the couch.

Precious's death happened thirteen years ago. His sympathy isn't necessary, but when his strong arms wrap around me and his lips linger on my hair after he tucks my head against his chest, I don't push him away.

I melt into the comfort he offers. The beat of his heart. The heat of his embrace.

And inside me, something ruffles.

Like the wings of a long-injured bird, desperate to take flight again.

day 3

three fence posts

December 28

chapter 7

[Pear]

Things got a little intense last night and my nerves prickle with dread at the thought of facing Brock this morning. After my deep confession about my sister, I suggested we watch a movie and pushed open the dove-decorated panels to reveal a flat-screen television behind the doors. Dad built a slim box to contain the modern device above the antiquated fireplace.

Brock agreed to watch holiday rom-coms, despite Christmas having passed, and we picked apart every cheesy statement and lacking plotline. After such a heavy discussion, the laughter felt good even at the expense of weak acting and even weaker on-screen chemistry. We criticized how unrealistic each representation was about budding relationships. Brock was exceptionally good at predicting what the men would say, and even better at determining the overall storyline within the first few minutes.

But even spoiling the plot and mocking the characters, I admitted to loving every awkward moment and scandalous last-second kiss (said with full mockery) like a pearl-clutching ninny tee-heeing from a rush of arousal.

The movies were further proof of my hope and belief that true love exists.

When I went to bed, I'd realized I'd come to a small town, although not my hometown, lost and seeking clarity, where I've met a rugged man who wears flannels, or at least he had earlier in the day. However, we aren't trying to save a farm, family business or bakery, and he doesn't own a dog. That I know of.

Two out of four isn't bad but we aren't the type of couple viewers would root for.

The thought gives me another giggle in the morning as I walk toward the kitchen, enticed by a heavenly smell. Emerging from the hallway, I stop short when I see syrup and butter on the dining table set with two plates.

"You made breakfast?" I glance up to see Brock wearing jeans and the requisite flannel shirt. He looks as delicious as the kitchen smells.

"Hope you like French toast."

How did he know my favorite? And when a plate with three perfect triangular slices sprinkled with powdered sugar and cinnamon are set on the table for me, I could kiss him. No mistletoe required.

"Are you feeling okay?" He's being awfully nice to me. Flowers yesterday. Grocery shopping. Watching holiday movies. Now breakfast. "What do you want?"

Brock falters beside the table, staring back at me. "I didn't know it was a crime to make breakfast."

"It's not. It's just . . ." I'm not used to someone—a man—being so nice to me. Not that people are generally rude or openly mean, but his thoughtfulness goes above and beyond while serving a twelve-day sentence. And whenever Reggie wanted something or he'd done something he knew I wasn't going to like, he'd be nice for a few hours. Like make me breakfast.

Brock watches me for a long minute, waiting on me to further explain myself, but I don't. Instead, I lower onto a chair. "Thank you."

The two simple words make his smile grow three sizes larger. His grin should come with a warning because those dark eyes brighten, and the curve of his mouth is sinful. He nods, allowing me another pass on sharing a snowflake story, as he calls my history. Busying himself with a mug of coffee and a hot chocolate for me, he brings both mugs to the table before he takes a seat across from me.

Without much preamble, he starts shoveling in his food like a man who hasn't eaten in weeks. Out of the corner of my eye, I catch the vase of white tulips I placed on the center of the table last night. There's a contrast between the delicate petals, the blossoms still closed tight, and the powerful hand lifting food on a fork to feed himself. I don't know what the dichotomy means but I don't try to analyze it.

Instead, I dig into French toast and hum with pleasure as I taste the breakfast Brock made for me.

+ + +

"So, I noticed these busted fence posts on my run the other day, and they need to be repaired."

Brock and I stand at the corner of an area marked off by wooden posts and wire fencing between the orchard and the neighboring property. The morning is surprisingly sunny and crisp but not biting. Snow still covers the ground as the sun can only do so much to melt the blanket laid down days ago. More snow is predicted in the coming days so getting this fence fixed feels like a must.

"Afraid the cows will get out," Brock mocks, knowing we don't have any cows at the orchard.

"Nope. More worried about them getting in."

"What?" Brock stands upright from his crouched position inspecting the posts that are practically snapped in half.

"The neighbor has cows, and they are free to roam. Scared the heck out of me when I was coming down the lane one morning and a giant heifer wandered into my path."

Brock chuckles at the image as I recall the black and white beast that stepped before me, moo-ing at me like I was in her way.

"Should come with a warning bell, huh?"

"Something like that." I smile. "So the fence posts . . ."

"Typically, you'd dig out the old post and replace it with a new one, but this ground is frozen solid, and an average post-hold digger won't get you anywhere. I'd suggest a trip to a home improvement store for some lumber and maybe some new wires as a temporary fix."

"That works."

We need to take Brock's truck, and when we enter it, he notices the absence of a car for me.

"How did you get here?"

"I Ubered to my aunt's house to surprise my dad on Christmas Day, hoping to spend some time with him between the holidays. Surprise was on me, though, because he wouldn't be here for the next two weeks. He'd probably told me, and I'd just spaced on it." I'd had a lot on my mind recently.

"And you didn't rent one?" Brock's brows pinch. "How would you get somewhere if I wasn't here?"

I shrug. "I hadn't considered going anywhere. You can get almost anything you need delivered nowadays."

His expression hardens. Jaw tightening. I can almost hear his thoughts, going into dad mode. *What would you do in an emergency?* If I were in a state of emergency, I probably wouldn't be able to drive anyway. Plus, my car was being shipped to Chicago, due for delivery any day, but I wasn't ready to share this information with Brock.

Finding what we needed at the home improvement store was relatively easy. However, Brock refused to let me pay for the items and we spent ten minutes arguing about how he wasn't responsible for the expense of the fence, only fixing it. To which he countered that he'd invoice Dad later for the money.

We were eventually interrupted when a worker asked if we needed help and when we both declined rather adamantly, the older man didn't flinch. He chuckled instead.

"How long you been married?"

Brock and I blink, glancing at one another before turning in tandem to the man.

"Nothing like home improvement projects to spark an argument. But once that honey-do project is done, she'll make it up to you, am I right?" He winks at me, but I'm still too floored by his assumption that Brock and I are a couple to respond.

Brock claps the man on the shoulder in a display of good ol' boys' club bonding, while side-eyeing me and guffawing. "Oh, she's going to make it up to me."

My mouth falls open, but Brock reaches for the edge of the lumber cart and pushes it forward, leaving me a second behind him with the store worker.

"Thirty-seven years with my misses. Worth every fight." Fondness fills his voice.

Marriage is work. It has its moments. It has its rewards.

I glance at Brock's back, or rather his backside, as he tilts forward pushing the lumber cart.

Would every fight with him be worth it?

Something tells me it might.

$+++$

Brock sheepishly asks for my assistance with the fence posts. While the work could be done by one, having an extra set of hands would help and I'm feeling generous today. The sun is still shining brightly, and I take a deep inhale of the fresh wintery air around us.

After our silly spat, we chatted easily about anything but fences on our return to the farm. Brock likes hard rock music from the eighties; I'm a country fan. He likes espionage films; we've already established I like holiday rom-coms. Which leads to a discussion about *Die Hard* being a Christmas classic . . . or not. And whether *Harry Potter and the Order of the Phoenix* should be included in holiday movie debates.

"It should," Brock adamantly argues.

"You've watched *Harry Potter* movies?" I don't know why I'm surprised.

We've driven as close as we could to the broken fencing and Brock hardly gives me a glance, concentrating on the first fence post while he answers. "My daughter Ellie was a huge fan. She's the Hermione-type. Know-it-all, smart as a whip, heart of gold."

Delight fills his voice as he speaks of his daughter.

"Wants to be a teacher when she graduates."

"A noble profession. And what about your son?"

The tool in his hand slips and Brock pauses, staring at the post before him. "He's a good kid." He sighs. "I rode him hard in high school. Wanted him to take advantage of every opportunity at school. Work hard. Play football harder. Wanted him to get a scholarship."

"And did he?"

"Yeah." Pride fills Brock's voice once more, but something strained mingles with his proud papa tone. He snorts. "But he doesn't really know what he wants. Says he wants to be a fireman."

"A noble profession as well," I remind him.

Brock shakes his head. "I know but I just want . . . I don't know . . ." Brock stands and runs his knuckles underneath his chin. "I want him to do something more. Something that would bring him more money. More stability. Less risk."

"What about happiness? Isn't that important?"

"A job's a job." Brock squints and glances off into the distance.

"Are you unhappy with the department?"

His head swivels and his eyes narrow at me. "Are you trying to head shrink me again?"

"No." Taken aback by his sharp tone and sudden change in demeanor, I stare at him.

Maybe I'm referring more to myself. My job had been *just* a job and I'd wanted something more for myself. I didn't know what that would be any better than Brock's college-age son, or so it seemed. For me, I hadn't been able to stomach one more day in Atlanta. I had no idea what was next for me.

In answer to Brock's question, I wanted him to be more open-minded. "So what if your son wants to be a fireman? Let him learn for himself if he loves or hates the job. Let him discover if it's a job or his life's calling. Let him be his own person."

Brock huffs, eyes still aimed toward the opposite farmland. The silence around us turns as cold as the air.

"Is this about you and your family? Your sense of obligation and the responsibility you took to be there for them when you were young."

"What?" His head whips in my direction, eyes aimed at me, hot like burning coal.

"Your son doesn't need to step up like you did, and that's a good thing, right? But that doesn't mean he's stepping down by being what he wants to be."

"He's twenty years old and talking about quitting school for the department. He doesn't know what he wants."

"Neither do I at times, and I'm forty-one." Forget that I've just given up a job and have no plans for the future.

"You're an adult," Brock grunts.

"But he's not a kid." Maybe he wasn't a gainfully employed adult, living on his own, and providing for himself, but he's not a child. He has choices. *His* choices, and he needs to make them for himself.

Suddenly, I'm twenty-two myself, recalling conversations with my dad about being my own person, and not always Precious's twin. I didn't begrudge being a twin, but she was more dynamic than me. Social. Outgoing. And I'd been in her shadow ever since she was born three minutes before me.

Unfortunately, with the loss of my sister came some of the first choices I made for myself, resulting in a move to Atlanta and an engagement to Reggie. Both mistakes, but mistakes I had to make on my own.

"And you're not a parent."

The blow claws into my chest like it was delivered by the notched hammer he's holding.

"You're right," I whisper, defeat in my tone but heat wrapped around the admission. With a nod, I drop the board I'd been holding for Brock, waiting on his instructions, and stalk toward his truck.

"Pear," he calls after me, but I'm done with this man today. Hot and cold. Up and down. I want off the emotionally loaded, careening out of control sleigh ride.

I should send him packing. Instead, I stomp toward the lane leading back to the house and see myself off. He can fix the three fence posts on his own. Maybe he'll have time to reflect on his family.

From the sounds of it, he has some mending to do there as well.

day 4

four calling bird(houses)

December 29

chapter 8

[Brock]

Yesterday, I'd messed up. Like royally fucked up. Pear and I had a great time the other night watching movies and drinking too much. Then yesterday morning, her face beamed when I made her breakfast. Those blue eyes as bright as the day. Her cherry-red lips curling like a Cheshire cat, all sultry but sweet. Fuck, when she looked at me like that, the way my heart hammered could crack my chest. Even walking through the home improvement store and setting up to repair a fence in the freezing cold did nothing to cool the warmth inside me as we spent time together.

But then we had to talk about my son, Nick, and I went too far. Damn mouth. Running off the rails again.

Pear wasn't being intrusive. She was more inquisitive, like she really wanted to know why I was so reactive and why I rode my son about his future. She might not be a parent, but that didn't mean she didn't understand that making the wrong decision when you are young could mess up everything.

I didn't want that for Nick.

I wanted more for both of my kids.

When I finally finished the fence after hammering my own thumb three times, cutting my hand on the cold wiring, and feeling a numbness in my fingertips, I'd wanted nothing more than to call my kids and hear their voices. Unfortunately, today was the day of Melissa and Kennedy's wedding. I passed on calling as the kids would be too busy to talk to their old man.

When I returned to a cold living room and quiet house, my mood remained at a simmer.

Without a car, Pear didn't have the means to leave. Still, I panicked when she didn't respond to the knock on her bedroom door. What if something happened to her on her walk back to the house? What if a cow had already gotten into the orchard?

The ridiculous thought had me cracking open her door to find her curled up on the bed, a blanket over her legs, a book near her head.

I didn't want to disturb her, although I owed her an apology. Maybe more flowers were in order, but Pear seemed like the type who would be offended further by flowers. Petals on stems didn't say I'm sorry to her. She'd want action, not reaction; only I didn't know what that should look like.

And it shouldn't have been something I'd lost sleep over, but I did.

My night was restless with thoughts of Pear and my kids. Maybe she was right about Nick. He didn't have the same pressures I'd had. In many ways, he had it so much easier, and I wanted him to take advantage of the opportunities he'd been given. I didn't want him to blow off his scholarship. He was a student athlete. He'd earned his scholarships and worked hard for his position on the college team. He had so much ahead of him.

Still, there was something to be said for happiness, and I'd been happy with the department. Sure, the ride has been bumpy at times, but I loved being a firefighter. A noble profession, Pear called it. She wasn't wrong. I wanted Nick to be proud of whatever he did, to feel accomplished at something.

However, I wasn't certain the department was the place for him. Then again, the hesitation might be my fear. I don't want to ever get the news my kid has died in a blaze. Having to witness the deep loss in parents' eyes at firemen funerals is rough. I don't want to be on the receiving end of that kind of pain.

To my surprise, Pear is gone in the morning, but another note telling me to meet her in the workshop is propped up against a red mug positioned next to the perking coffeepot.

"Good morning," I mutter, as I enter the cold building. While the wood-burning stove is on, the space hasn't heated up yet. Neither has the air around Pear.

"Mornin'," she mumbles, lifting an awkwardly large box that looks a little too heavy for her onto a make-shift worktable consisting of a sturdy piece of wood resting over two sawhorses.

"What's the plan today?" Infusing my voice with more enthusiasm than I feel, I hope to crack the ice between us.

"Owl boxes."

With blinking eyes, I stare at the sturdy flat box on the worktable.

"We need to build them and hang them."

"We?" I arch a brow, surprised she's willing to help me today.

"There are four of them and it will take all day if you do this alone."

"Where do they need to be hung?"

"We can affix one to the outside of the barn. Two on posts that once belonged to bird feeders, and the last one will go on a dead tree on the edge of the property near the forest."

"Why not install some simple birdhouses?"

Pear stops moving and finally looks at me. "Because my dad likes owls." *End of discussion.*

On that note, I rip open the edge of one box while Pear opens another, and we begin the tedious process of matching parts and pieces. A goes into slot A while supported by B in the B-hole. I'd laugh if I wasn't growing more and more agitated with the strained, tense silence between us.

Her unwillingness to talk right now speaks volumes and I have a strange itch to communicate with her, when communication has never been a strength of mine.

Eventually, Pear slams the instructions in her hand against a square piece of flat wood and hangs her head. "There isn't enough space for the two of us."

The table is cramped and with each of us trying to keep our distance, an invisible line exists that divides the already tight table into even smaller halves.

"My place or yours, then?" I suggest, hinting at the owls' intended new homes. "I'll help you with yours, if you'll help me with mine."

Pear scowls at me, eyes narrowing like I have some kind of agenda in building owl boxes.

"Fine," she mutters.

"Fine," I counter, but a smile tugs at the corner of my mouth. At least we'll be talking even if it's put part C into slot C.

I move the panels I'd been working with onto the flattened cardboard of the open box and set everything on the floor before stepping beside Pear, awaiting her instructions.

She holds up a long, rectangular piece of wood and lifts a side panel. "Part A slides into the A-hole."

And with that, we're both cracking up and the tension between us slowly breaks.

+ + +

Driving my truck around the property, we hang the boxes in the places Pear suggested. The owl boxes were heavy as hell and awkward as shit to carry up a ladder one-handed but the smile on Pear's face after each box is in place is worth it.

Once finished, she stands back to admire each creation, like I'd built *her* a home. Little gleams of light sparked in her eyes despite the midwinter day growing dark at an early hour. Standing in the shadow of my headlights, her body outlined by the brightness, I wanted nothing more than to kiss her.

"Think owls will really nest in there?" I ask.

With her hands still covered in mittens but tucked under her chin, Pear stares up at the two houses we installed last. The ones on the old birdfeeder posts.

"We're a little late to set them up. They should have been hung in October, but I read you can go as late as February and owls will still find their new homes." She pauses a second. "But I don't know why an owl wouldn't love that place." She nods at the box on a thick column. "It looks inviting, right? If I were an owl, I'd want to live there."

I chuckle at the thought of her living in a box suspended in the air. If she lived there, I'd want to live there as well.

"February? Don't tell me. Owls are the official birds of Valentine's Day, like jars of pears are the official fruit."

"Definitely official bird of romance," she teases. "Nothing says love like the hoot of an owl."

I snort, and without thinking, wrap my arm around her and kiss the side of her head. We make a great pair, whether she agrees or not.

Once back inside the warm *human* house, Pear cooks dinner for us even though she grumbled only days ago about feeding me. I hadn't intended for her to provide anything for me, but I am grateful all the same. I can cook but I don't love it. Breakfast is my specialty.

Dinners are typically a quick affair for me. Now that I'm alone, with both kids in college, I eat most of my evening meals standing at the kitchen counter, scrolling my phone while rushing through what I consider a necessity more than a pleasure.

Pear, on the other hand, enjoys every meal. She savors each bite, talking between each sample. A meal is an occasion for her. Tonight, we have pork chops she slow-cooked in mesquite barbeque sauce all day with a side of roasted potatoes, and I don't think I've ever eaten anything so delicious in my life.

Pear is an amazing cook. *Baker* and cook. Her pie was heavenly. Her pork chops divine. I'll happily take anything she wants to make me. Not that I wouldn't cook for her. I can't wait to tackle that tenderloin I bought. We've agreed to save it for New Year's Eve, the official halfway mark of my stay.

The days are passing quickly, and the thought of leaving creates a strange ache behind my sternum.

"You okay?" Pear asks, catching me while I rub my knuckles over my breastbone.

"Heartburn," I lie.

"You eat too fast."

I sigh, falling back in my seat and staring at my empty plate. "Hazard of an empty nest. I eat alone a lot and hardly ever sit at my table. No reason to slow down. Just eat and move on."

"Eat and be done. *Blasphemy*." A sweet smile curls her mouth as she scolds me.

We're finally back to the easiness that has developed between us over the last four days, and I, for one, am relieved. I *like* her, and I want her to like me. Not like some teenage crush thing, but actually enjoy my company, as a man. A man who hasn't been with a woman in a long time. A man who values friendship but also wants more.

I'm not certain Melissa was my friend. We told each other things, but did we listen to one another? Did we hear what the other wanted? What the other needed? Melissa hadn't heard my desire to build furniture. She'd scoffed at the idea. *Guess carpentry was even lower on her list than fireman*. Funny how being who I am never bothered her at first. Eventually, who I am led to a nice house. A decent car. Private education for our kids. It's also strange she then ended up with a fire*woman* as her partner.

After the divorce from my wife and dissolution of my friendship with Kenny, Kenny took a position in a suburban fire department.

"Did you hear that?" Pear pauses, fork midway to her lips.

"What?" I tilt my head, listening.

"That—" Pear is already pushing back her chair, forgetting about her unfinished dinner and rushing toward the front door.

"Where are you going?" I laugh as she struggles to tug her coat off the hook.

"Outside." She giggles like a boy-band-crushing teen while she steps into a pair of boots without bothering to lace them up and tugs on a jacket, skipping the zipper. Jamming her knit cap on her head, she opens the front door and steps outside, gingerly crossing the porch.

I stand to follow her, stopping within the open doorway, and then I hear it.

Ah-who-who-who.

"Oh my God."

"Shh," Pear shushes, turning toward me with a finger to her lips before swiveling back toward the barn. We hung the box on the eastern side to protect the creature from the harsh winds that rush off the lake and make this region in Michigan a snowbelt. Still, I'm shocked an owl has found the home so quickly.

While sliding my feet into my construction boots, I pull my jacket off the coat hook I designated as my own. I shove my arms into my coat, tugging the door to close behind me. The soft click sounds too loud in the silence of the night.

Pear hushes. "We must be very quiet."

"Because we're hunting wabbits," I whisper.

Pear scowls which proves she gets the reference. Elmer Fudd would be proud.

Once we cautiously step onto the gravel drive, Pear walks gingerly, her pace slow as she circles the barn. The moment feels like we are kids playing ghosts in the graveyard or hide and seek, sneaking up on an unsuspecting friend.

Pear pauses again when she hears the distinct cry.

Ah-who-who-who.

The hoot is throaty and strong. His call sounds weary but wise.

"He's staking his claim," Pear whispers. "He's warning other owls to stay away."

"Really?"

"Or he could be calling to a mate."

"You seem to know a lot about owls."

"I told you, my dad loves them." Pear turns her head to face me. Her hands are stuffed in her coat pocket while her jacket remains open.

Stepping closer to her, I shift her and zip up her coat, tugging the hood over her head. She tips her head back and looks up at the sky.

"I love nights like this," she states quietly, as if she'll disturb the absolute silence. "The moon casts everything in a blue light."

I hadn't noticed, too curious about the owl, and concerned about following Pear.

Turning my head, I see what she means. Everything glows in a dull blue-gray gleam while the sky is an inky black and the moon a vibrant white disc. The silence around us even takes on a color, like the white noise of snowflakes floating to the ground.

"It's beautiful," I whisper to the heavens, breathing in the crisp, cool air. A chill runs down the back of my neck, yet I'm not cold. Something about this night feels magical, mystical maybe. A mystery is being shared with me, and I'm trying to listen. I want to learn the secret. I hear something but I can't make out what I'm being told.

Instead, I face Pear again, who is watching me.

"Yeah. Beautiful," she whispers as her warm eyes meet mine.

"I'm sorry about yesterday," I say, not really wanting to discuss yesterday's tension in the midst of our present peace, but something inside me begs me to seek her forgiveness.

"Me, too. It's not my place—" She stops as my finger covers her lips.

"Do you hear that?" I cup my ear.

"What?" Her voice drops low, and she tips her head to the side as if she'll hear better.

"*Ah-who-who-who,*" I call out, quiet but deep.

"What are you doing?" She giggles, covering her mouth to quell the sudden noise. Only, I want to hear her laughter. I want to see her smile. And I want to taste her mouth.

Pulling at strands of her hair that peek out from beneath her cap and hang straight against her shoulder, I say, "I'm staking my claim."

Or maybe I'm making a mating call. *Be mine. Be mine. Be mine.*

I certainly understand how owls might work romantically during Valentine's.

I'd prefer, if their call had an effect, on December twenty-ninth. A random Thursday in early winter.

And when Pear tips up on her toes and brushes my lips with a light kiss, I'm not certain I've ever been more surprised.

With a kiss as soft as an owl's feather, she's claimed me. And I don't know if I've ever been happier.

day 5

five rusty runners

December 30

chapter 9

[Pear]

Our mouths press together with the softest of touch. Caught up in the moonlight and the moment, I worried I'd gone too far.

I'm staking my claim.

Did he mean me? With only four days of knowing him, he couldn't possibly.

Still, when I lower to my heels and pull back from his mouth, he catches me by the back of my head, and our eyes lock a second before he leans forward to kiss me this round.

And Brock Scroggs knows how to kiss a woman.

After the open-mouth kisses and tongue licking on my neck two days ago, I already had a sense of how he'd kiss but this was different. Soft while insistent. Eager but patient. Tender while teasing. His lips caress mine, guiding them to follow his lead. His tongue doesn't press forward. His teeth don't nip. Only his mouth controls this moment and from the top of my head to the tips of my toes I feel him everywhere. I've never been kissed like this.

With purpose. With restraint. With care.

Brock is on a mission to melt my insides, or rather, heat them up. However, he takes things no further than this simplistic kiss before he pulls back and rests his forehead against mine.

"Thank you," he whispers in the silent night.

"For what?" I smile, wanting to thank him for such a kiss, for igniting a flame within me. For waking me up inside.

"For giving me a chance." His honesty hints that Brock hasn't been given many opportunities to prove his worth. Or maybe he's been trying to prove himself worthy too often.

"I'd give you a dozen," I admit.

"Twelve days, right?"

That actually wasn't what I meant, but I smile all the same.

His comment is a reminder that we only have twelve days together. Soon, he'll go back to Chicago, and I'll . . . still be here wondering what I'm going to do next with my life.

+ + +

On the fifth day of Brock's stay, I have a difficult task for him.

"Five rusty runners," I announce, after pulling back the giant tarp on one of two items in the old barn.

"Is that a—" He states the make and model number of the snowmobile so fast I don't have any idea what he's said.

I'm also not certain if it's rust or just wear and tear on the sliders that propel the snowmobile like wheels on a vehicle, but they need to be cleaned or replaced.

"Can we take it out for a spin?" Like an eager child wanting to ride a new bike, Brock's face is lit with excitement.

"Why don't you inspect it first. I'm not certain it even has the proper gas." I pause a second realizing I might have made an assumption that Brock would understand the mechanics of a snowmobile. Plus, if parts need to be replaced, I have no idea where to find them locally.

"I also have this project for you."

Pulling back the tarp on a second item, which catches at first because of its height compared to mine, Brock gasps once more.

"Is that an actual sleigh? Like a horse drawn one?"

"Yep." Glee fills my voice. "The sleigh came with the house, and for years I've been begging my dad to polish the runners and the box and take this beautiful old thing out for a run."

I wanted to take an honest to goodness sleigh ride in the snow.

"You don't have horses," Brock states the obvious. We don't, and Dad wasn't confident he could steer them even if he could rent some from a local farm.

"Neither here nor there." I dismiss his observation. We're putting the sleigh before the horses, so to speak, but I wanted this carriage spiffed up and shining for Dad. And me. Mostly me.

"Do you know anything about sleighs? Or snowmobiles?"

Brock pulls up his phone. "I'll learn because I want to drive that thing." He nods at the modern machinery while I sigh over the antique vehicle.

Brock and I couldn't be more opposite, but then I recall our kiss last night and realize we fit.

Like peppermint and chocolate. One sweet and sugary, the other smooth and creamy; both delicious on their own, but decadent when mixed together.

+ + +

While Brock works diligently during the day, I tackle removing my dad's Christmas tree.

The holiday season was my mother's delight and my sister's demise, so Dad and I struggled for a long time on how to navigate this time of year. Eventually, I'd thrown myself into Reggie's orbit and allowed myself to be swallowed into his family's traditions when I secretly missed my own. Once I divorced Reggie, I returned home two years in a row to find this old farmhouse dripping in holiday cheer.

Dad had come to terms with the season and the reason for it. He believed light came out of the dark moments, and we needed to honor both. The bright memories of my mother and sister, and their quiet, lingering absence.

This year, I didn't think I would make it home. Work was a bitch. There was no other term for Eat 'em Industries. The final straw had been the lack of bonuses for the second year in a row after months of working overtime. As a salaried executive, I wasn't eligible for the benefit of additional pay for the extra hours I put in, so I looked forward to the bonus as compensation. I had plans for the money; a cushion of security I hadn't had in years. However, Eat 'em failed me, and I was simply tired of their changing company policies and lacking moral code.

Coming home to surprise my dad hadn't been on my agenda, but once I'd given notice at Eat 'em and set things in motion to make another major change in my life, I couldn't wait to get here. I couldn't wait to talk to him. Tell him the truth about Reggie and my struggles over the past few years. Tell him my plan to live closer to him. The hardest part would be confessing that I didn't have a clue what I'll do next.

Finding the house dripping in holiday ornamentation was a warm welcome, almost like a sign that the decisions I'd made were the right ones. I was where I needed to be, and I'd been absent for too long.

With silent nostalgia and a tug in my heart, I remove each ornament from the tree, wrapping them in tissue and restoring them to the proper storage bin for next year. Dad doesn't mind leaving his tree up for the full twelve days of Christmas. Tradition demands it. Some religions do, too. But I like a clean house to start the new year, and with tomorrow being New Year's Eve, I want the tree removed. However, I'm not ready to remove the festive garland or fairy lights along the mantel that light up the room, giving off a soft glow and cozy ambiance.

When Brock finally enters the house, looking agitated, it's dark outside. Sometimes I think that irritated scowl and hard jawline is simply his look. He's handsome despite it, but devastatingly good-looking when he smiles. I like his mouth. The smirky curl when he fights a smile. The widening of his lips when he grins. The flash of white teeth, suggesting he's up to something mischievous. The way those lips taste against mine.

"What's wrong?" I ask, watching as he brushes snow off his coat and tugs off his knit hat. Not going to lie, I've had fantasies of him wearing only that gray cap and his jeans minus anything else.

"Why does something need to be wrong?"

"It doesn't *need* to be. You just look grouchy."

His bushy brows lift at my assessment. "I think it's just my natural disposition."

"But it's not," I laugh. "You have a nice smile."

The compliment pulls his lips upward, hitching one side higher than the other. I hold my breath, anticipating what will appear next. The hint of white teeth flash at me. Along with the flare of his teeth, his cheeks pinken deeper than the dash of cold on them.

Is he blushing? Brock Scroggs is actually flushed by a compliment, and I suddenly want to give him a dozen of them.

"I, uh, I found an extra set of slides for the snowmobile in the barn, but I had trouble with them, and the job took me longer than I anticipated. I won't know for certain if I have them properly installed until I can take the snowmobile for a run. As for the sleigh . . ." Brock drops his gaze. "It's more than I can tackle. The runners look like they need a lot of sanding, possibly sandblasting, and then a coat of rust protection to seal them. I didn't find a sandblaster among Cap's tools, and the barn is too cold for coating even if I found the bonder I'd need."

He hasn't removed his coat yet and with his knit cap in his hand, nervously being twirled around and around, his head hangs lower as if he's nervous because he hasn't completed today's task. Or maybe he feels incompetent by not being able to do the job. Something he would have called stupid days ago. Maybe he even did, cursing the project several times while out in the barn.

"It's okay," I tell him, softening my voice and slowly approaching him. "What matters is you tried. We can't always complete every task in a day. And sometimes projects are bigger than we can tackle. Mentally or physically."

Brock nods, still not lifting his head. "I just don't want to disappoint Cap." I see his Adam's apple bob when he adds, "Or you."

"You haven't disappointed me, fireman." Sure, I'd love to see that old sleigh in working order, but the antique runners need a lot more work than I anticipated.

Brock nods once more, finally lifting his head higher but avoiding my eyes as he slips off his coat and hangs it on a hook like he's part of our very small family. The camel-colored jacket looks right at home among the other jackets and scarves hanging off the hooks, and when

Brock kicks off his boots, but places them in a cubby hole beneath the bench, I marvel at their rightness there as well.

He might need this farmhouse as much as me to know he's welcome and worthy.

"I'll Be Home For Christmas" plays on the small sound system Dad has installed in the kitchen area. I'd been listening to a holiday playlist as my final farewell to the Christmas season, and suddenly my eyes well with tears.

Instantly, Brock is before me. His brows pinch in question but he doesn't ask. Instead, he takes my hand and gently pulls me closer to him. To the sound of Bing Crosby crooning, we sway in the space between the dining table and the living room.

For too long, being home has been a dream. Living closer to my dad. Returning to myself.

But now I'm here. Where I'm meant to be.

Maybe Brock is meant to be here, too.

day 6

six balls a dropping

December 31

chapter 10

[Pear]

I wake to a fresh layer of snow covering the ground and no sign of it letting up anytime soon. However, the day isn't completely gray.

"I've decided today should be a cheat day," I announce as we eat oatmeal sprinkled with cinnamon and a dash of milk for breakfast on the morning of New Year's Eve.

"You're springing the inmate?" Brock teases. His beard has grown fuller since his arrival. The white more prominent than the black and complementing his hair which is more ink than silver. Despite being indoors, he's wearing a baseball cap, backwards. And I want to climb him like a chimney.

"I'm giving you a rest. Besides I had six gates a leanin' on the list, but after the fence posts, I realize winter isn't the best time to repair fencing."

Brock sits up straighter. "But is there still something that needs to be done?"

"Another day." I wave, appreciating his concern, almost eagerness, but dismissing it.

"So, today's plan is . . ."

"Snowmobiling."

He pauses, his spoon suspended in midair. "Are you serious?" He sounds like a kid given the present he wanted most for Christmas.

His enthusiasm forces the smile on my face to grow. "You worked hard on fixing the slides and you mentioned needing to test them. I'm certain Dad has a pair of snow bibs that would fit you." I'm not certain what Brock will do about footwear as his construction boots won't cut it in the billowing drifts, but he hasn't appeared to care.

"This will be amazing. I can't remember the last time I went snowmobiling." Suddenly, he's shoveling down the oatmeal he earlier protested, warning me he wasn't an oatmeal kind of guy. Apparently, he's a new fan.

"Okay, fireman. Slow down."

He stills a second, pausing the swirl of his spoon around the oversized mug, and stares directly at me. "I just want to clarify, I'm not a cheater, even if we have a cheat day."

Surprised by this admission, I blink twice. "Of course."

His gaze holds on my face. "I'm loyal to a fault, I guess. It's why I want to prove myself to Cap. The department is where I want to be. Where I want to stay."

I nod once. "Totally understandable. Your secret is safe with me." I wink.

Dad won't need to know we took a day off. In fact, explaining all the days is going to be difficult, but that's a problem for day thirteen. Not today.

After Brock's bold statement, he rushes to finish the rib-coating meal and rinse out his mug. Then he disappears into Dad's room to change into layers of clothes. I, on the other hand, take my time to finish my yummy oatmeal and sip my hot chocolate, once again laced with peppermint.

"What are you doing?" Brock questions as he returns to the main room.

I stare back at him, my lacking comprehension evident.

"Get dressed," he commands.

"Oh, I'm not—" Adamantly shaking my head, I brush off the idea of me on a snowmobile.

"It's like riding a motorcycle."

"I don't ride those either."

"Ever?"

"Never."

Brock stares at me, his expression blank. "Why not?"

I shrug. "Guess the opportunity has never presented itself."

"Well, consider this"—he pats on his chest—"as an opportunity knocking. Get dressed."

"I don't—"

"Get. Dressed." The command might be non-threatening, but there's a warning in his rugged voice. He's not arguing with me.

I'm in no rush to dress, and use the bathroom three times for good measure as I'll have layers and layers of clothing on and no desire to remove it for outdoor peeing. When I'm finally ready, an impatiently waiting Brock is nearly bursting out of his skin. Pacing, he fights to stay calm as I lace up my boots and zip up my jacket.

"Ready," I announce.

"Finally," he mutters. Then he winks.

Snow is falling lightly but collecting on top of the already accumulated drifts as we make our way to the barn. Brock runs a series of quick checks on the snowmobile, explaining how he found gas in a portable can, and our first mission is to find a gas station to fill the tank.

When he hops on the motorized sled, he revs the throttle and waits for me to climb on. With the abundance of clothing between us, I wouldn't expect to feel the strength of his body once I'm seated, but I do. Climbing behind him is like I imagine riding a motorcycle would be. With my arms wrapped around him, I discover his mid-section is tight. His legs are powerful against the inside of my thighs. The vibration beneath does nothing to quell the desire rising every day for this man.

"Hang on," he hollers over the loud engine.

Brock guides us along the lane before cutting between the dormant pear trees for thicker pillows of snow. He drives with caution, which I assume is for my benefit, as he navigates us through the orchard and toward a main road in search of a gas station.

Once our tank is full, Brock pays inside the station and returns to the snowmobile with a swaggering stride. "The attendant told me about a nearby trail. Ready for a ride?"

I could snark that he hadn't given me an option but it's clear he's offering me a choice now.

I only nod and watch as Brock blinds me with another one of his hard-won grins. He's so good looking, even with layers of clothing and a helmet on his head.

He climbs back on the snowmobile, and we take off for trails that weave and curl through the woods. I have no idea how Brock knows where we are going, but I eventually stop wondering and give in to the beauty of nature around us. Despite the roar of the engine, it's peaceful among the snow-laden trees and the thickly laid snow paths. Underneath the heavy canopy of towering evergreens and deciduous trees now absent of leaves, the falling snow isn't as prevalent, but the effects of the overnight flakes have made their mark. With ice coated branches and strips of downy snow on solid limbs, the forest truly is a winter wonderland.

"It's so beautiful," I holler, uncertain if Brock can hear me. When he doesn't answer, I assume he can't.

We blaze among the trees and trails for an undetermined amount of time before Brock finally slows to a stop.

"You okay?" he calls back to me.

"I'm great." I'm not certain I've ever felt so free. Free from worry. Free from cares. Sitting back and clinging to Brock feels reassuring. Like I don't need to be in charge. Like I can do anything I want. Later.

Another snowmobile approaches and slows beside us. The driver is a man with a young girl in a pink snowsuit behind him. When he flips up his visor, deep brown eyes appear.

"You guys alright?" he hollers over the hum of idling engines.

"Yeah," Brock calls back. "But do you know how to get to Paradise Farms from here?"

"Are we lost?" I cry out.

The other man shifts on his rumbling machine. "You can either turn back around and head back toward Red Cedar Highway, or I'm pretty certain that moving forward you'll eventually hit the outer edge of the property. Look out for the fencing."

Ah, the fencing. Maybe that explains the busted section more than wayward cows.

"Thanks, man," Brock says.

"Happy New Year," the guy replies, flipping his eye shield back in place and aiming his gaze over his shoulder to the girl behind him. She gives a hesitant wave before gripping the sides of the man's outwear as they take off again.

"Are we lost?" I repeat.

Brock removes a hand from the handlebars and rubs it over my covered thigh. "I've got us, snowflake."

Not the most reassuring response, but also, equally comforting. Brock isn't going to let us be lost in the woods. He isn't going to let us flounder like Reggie eventually did, leading me astray and believing lies he told me.

We aren't struggling, baby.

We aren't a lost cause.

I don't know why I'm thinking about Reggie, and I quickly release the unwanted memories as we whiz past trees and weave along the natural trail eventually ending up along a fence line I recognize, especially when I see the temporary posts Brock recently installed. The snow is really piling up and I have a better sense of its depth as we near the wire lines outlining Dad's land.

"If we follow this to the right, there's a gate down the way."

Only, I'm wrong. There isn't a gate, and we travel longer than I'd expected. Despite the layering of long underwear and leggings, plus snow bibs, thick socks and solid boots, the cold air is seeping through the padding, and I shiver inside my jacket.

I don't want to complain, but I'm really cold.

Time seems to slow, and not in a good way, as it feels like forever before a familiar house comes into view in the distance. Brock eventually finds one of the leaning gates I mentioned, though not the one I thought was close, and he pushes it open as best he can in the thick snow drift. The opening he creates is only big enough for the snowmobile to squeak through and Brock hops off the powerful machine once more to right the gate.

With a hand on my shoulder, he questions me. "You still okay?"

I nod, holding back any complaint.

Brock returns to the helm and speeds down the straight lane. In our new haste, I appreciate the easy pace he took during our earlier wanderings. With this clear breakaway, he's gunning the engine. I want to feel that sense of freedom I felt earlier, but instead, I huddle against his back, squeezing his middle tighter.

The turtle-scarf around my neck has slipped and icy air whips against my skin.

We're almost there.

Then the engine sputters and the snowmobile jolts.

"What's happening?" I ask.

"I think we're out of gas."

"Haven't you been monitoring the gauge?"

"Of course, which is why I wanted to return home."

My gaze flits to the house. Walking the remaining distance won't be that bad but we can't leave the snowmobile in the middle of the orchard.

On cue, the machine coughs out its last bit of energy and stalls.

"Fuck," Brock mutters, loud and clear despite the scarf around his neck and helmet over his head.

I shift, swinging my leg over the side and sliding off the back seat. My legs vibrate. My thighs tremble.

"What are you doing?" Brock wonders, remaining seated while glancing at me over his shoulder. His visor is flipped upward, and his cheeks are ruddy.

"We're going to have to push this back to the barn."

Brock eyes me up and down. "I can do it."

"But it will be faster with the two of us."

A shiver ripples up my back and I visibly shake out my arms, chasing off the chill.

"You're cold."

I don't respond. It's snowing harder than it was earlier, and suddenly, the surrounding orchard doesn't look like a wonderland as much as a menacing blizzard whistling through the shorter trees.

"Why don't you head back to the house? I'll push it."

"I'm not leaving you out here alone." And I don't want to argue. It's too cold to fight. Stepping up to one side of the snowmobile, I brace my hands on the handlebar.

Brock hesitates a second before slipping off the opposite side and mirroring my position. Together, we push the heavy machine, which thankfully slides along the mounting snow. Still the effort is difficult as the snow is soft, and the snowmobile feels like it's sinking.

"Just leave it," Brock hollers over the sharp sting of whipping snow.

"No." My back is going to hate me, but I push with all the strength I can muster while we make tedious progress until, finally, we shove the snowmobile into the barn.

+ + +

Once we return to the house, Brock is quick to start a fire to heat up the main room and suggests I take a shower.

"Honestly, I think I'm too tired for the effort." I really should shower to warm up my skin and loosen my bones, but I just want warm clothes and a seat in front of the growing flames. "You can go first."

Something in my expression must tell Brock I don't have it in me to fight with him, and he heads for the bathroom while I change with trembling limbs and shaky fingers into my comfy pair of high-waisted, loose-legged pants, and a fluffy mid-drift sweater.

With Brock still in the shower, I turn on the television in time to watch a recap of the clock striking midnight in Australia. Keeping the television on mute, I make myself a cup of hot chocolate and turn on the coffeemaker for Brock. Then I settle on the floor before the fireplace, feeling the heat of the blaze warm my skin. The room is still festive with the garland strung along the mantel and the fairy lights twinkling within the evergreen strands. But with the tree removed, Christmas is gone.

I sigh a little in relief.

Moments later, Brock appears, standing at the edge of the living room. Leaning into the corner where the hallway meets the living room, his hands are slipped into the pockets of his black joggers. He's wearing another waffle-weave shirt with the buttons at his throat open and the sleeves pushed up to his elbows. His hair is still damp. Even his beard glistens a little, like he stepped out of the shower and didn't fully dry off.

"I'm sorry about outside."

"Running out of gas?" My brows cinch. "It's not like you planned it to happen."

His gaze remains on me. "I should have watched the gauge better."

I stare up at him, knowing I accused him of not doing such a thing, but it really wasn't his fault.

"I was having too much fun," he adds.

"Me too," I offer, keeping my eyes on him.

"But you were cold."

I shrug.

"Why didn't you say anything earlier? We could have come back sooner."

I was lifting my mug of steaming cocoa to my lips but stop short and answer. "Because you *were* having fun. And so was I."

"Snowflake," he whispers, like he's confused by my explanation.

"The coffee machine is on."

He doesn't move. His eyes still focused on me. "You should really shower."

"I'm slowly warming up right here," I tell him, happy with my position before the fireplace. A blanket covers my lap. My hands are heating from holding the warm mug. The feeling in my cheeks is returning.

When Brock moves, I expect him to head for the kitchen and coffee. Instead, he walks toward me and folds down behind me. With his legs spread on either side of me, his hand comes to my back and the heat of his palm seeps through my sweater.

I shiver beneath his touch. Then I feel the hem of my sweater lifting and I turn my head only enough to glance over my shoulder. Preparing to question him when my lower back is exposed, I fall short of speaking when his warm fingertips tickle my skin. Deepening the pressure, he rubs upward underneath my sweater.

I straighten my spine and tremble again. A hum that cannot be helped escapes.

With that, Brock flattens his palm against my spine, lowering it before slipping around my side and skating over my belly. His fingers are warm, but his forearm is hot, like a heated log pressed against my middle. Leaning backward into his chest, I melt.

"I'm sorry you were cold." His voice is quiet near my ear. His breath is as warm as other parts of him and tickles my neck.

"It's winter," I remind him.

"But you stayed out there for me."

"I told you I was having fun." My voice is equally as quiet as his, the crackling of the fire the only sound as the television flickers above the mantel but remains muted.

"No. You stayed to help me. Every day you've been helping me."

"I didn't help with the fence."

Brock shakes his head and his jaw brushes against my ear, the bristle of his facial hair soft and tickling once more. With his forearm against my belly and his hand squeezing at my side, I nestle my back further into the warmth of his chest. He's like my personal heating blanket.

When his mouth lands on my neck, I still for a second and Brock's hold around me stiffens. But he must sense the moment I relax, or maybe it's that the next kiss has me melting once more. He isn't as enthusiastic as he was the other day when his mouth openly sucked at my flesh. This kiss is soft, delicate, peppering and sweet.

When I tilt my head, exposing more of my neck, the kisses turn more insistent. His mouth opens, hungrier. His teeth scrape, the pressure harder. His tongue feathers over my flesh.

I snap and twist in his arms so my shoulder leans against his chest and I can face him. Our eyes don't meet. Our mouths do instead. While the first kiss might be a test, a reminder of the other night standing outside beneath the moonlight, within seconds our mouths are moving faster, the tension building stronger.

Kissing Brock Scroggs is an experience. One I'm not likely to ever forget.

The arm once wrapped around my belly, now reaches around my back and his palm holds me firmly in place against him. I slip my hand underneath his shirt, my fingertips instantly sizzling at the contact with his abs.

"You're a furnace," I mutter into his mouth.

He only smiles before deepening our kiss. Tugging on my lower lip. Licking at the corner of my mouth. Nipping at my chin. He moves along my jaw and down my neck before palming my chin in one hand and drawing my mouth back to his.

My fingertips dig into his stomach muscles which flinch underneath my attention. My hands are my eyes, feeling my way over ripples and dips. My fingers brush along a trail of hair below his belly button.

Brock sucks in a breath before turning up the temperature on our kisses. Tongues clash. Teeth gnash. But our connection isn't a battle. The only fight we encounter is to stay connected.

I shift once more, tossing off the blanket over my legs and rotating to my knees before straddling his lap. All the while our mouths never leave one another's until I settle over his thighs and press the gap between my thighs against the hard wedge in his loose-fitting joggers.

We groan in unison. With an arm wrapped around his neck and my hand in his hair at the top of his head, I roll my hips against him. His hand slides up my back inside my sweater, and clutches at the back of my neck. His other hand cups my ass, tugging me tighter against him.

We moan once more as my hot core hits his steel length.

Then, I'm suddenly off him and he is standing, pacing a few steps away from me.

Staring at his back, I'm shocked by his sudden retreat. Breathlessly, I watch him move like a caged polar bear.

"Did I do something wrong?" My reaction strikes from old insincerities.

Brock swipes a hand through his hair, before holding his palm against the back of his neck a second as his other arm moves, adjusting himself in the front.

He turns his head only slightly and I can make out his profile in the glow of the fireplace. "You're perfect."

"Then, I don't understand." Perched on my hand to prop myself upright, I stare at his back. Hurt. Confused.

"I . . . I don't want to rush."

Still surprised by his rapid rejection, there's something in his tone that gives me pause. "There's no rush. We can do as little or as much as you want." I take a deep breath, hoping I don't sound desperate to take things further. "We can stop right here." I don't want to add *and pretend like this didn't happen* because in no way can I pretend Brock didn't just kiss the stuffing out of me. "And we don't have to do this again."

I swallow around the lump in my throat and fight the prickle of tears.

Brock fully turns to face me, and my eyes lower for the solid length evident below his waistband.

"I definitely want to do more of this." He points between us. "It's just—" His gaze shifts toward the fireplace. "I've missed kissing and I want to enjoy this a little bit longer."

A moment passes before things click in my head. "Are you saying you want to make out with me?"

His head whips back in my direction, his eyes roaming my face for sarcasm or teasing. Now would not be the moment to joke with Brock as the tension in his jaw remains evident and his stance mimics a bobcat ready to pounce.

Slowly, his shoulders lower and his expression softens. His gaze drops to the floor. "Yeah."

Like the rush of a thermometer, heat rockets from my core up through my belly and into my throat. His request is rather sweet. And I'd love to keep kissing him.

"Okay." My throat is still thick so the suggestion comes out like a croak.

"Yeah?" Those coal-colored eyes soften to liquid ink as his hands come to his hips, his erection still thick and taunting.

I eagerly nod and chew the corner of my lip.

Brock tips his head back and stares up at the ceiling. "I'm gonna need a minute, though."

"Take your time." I swipe a hand through my long hair. Maybe I should have showered after all, as my fingers get caught in the tangles from wearing a hat most of the morning.

I scoot closer to the couch and set my elbow into a cushion, holding my head in a way I give a quick glance to the muted television.

"It's midnight in Paris now," I say for no apparent reason.

A loud clap startles me, and I rock my head on my hand to watch Brock rub both his palms down his face. "Time."

"What?" I chuckle as he takes a large step toward me and lowers to his knees, crawling the last foot to close the distance between us. He hovers before me.

"Time. Like in tag. Midnight hits and we must kiss."

"Oh, we must, must we?" I giggle, reaching out to rub my palm over his bristly jaw.

Brock turns his head and presses a kiss to the center of my hand. "We must." He nods once.

"Only kissing," I state more as a reminder than a question.

His eyes shift to my lips. His mouth crushes mine in answer and I fall to my back at the sudden impact. Brock follows after me, one of his legs between mine, his thigh pressing hard at my center. A strong rhythm beats like the dong of a clock counting down to twelve.

"You aren't playing fair," I mutter against his mouth pressed to mine, because it's quite possible I could orgasm just from this kiss.

Brock's hand somehow landed on my waist, and he glides it over my hip and down the outer edge of my leg. Curling his fingers around the back of my knee, he hitches my leg upward, driving the flat of his thick leg deeper into my core.

"Could I make you come just from kissing you?"

"Oh God, Brock." Damn him if he can. Damn him if he doesn't.

His hand retreats from my knee, gliding around the curve of my thigh and the expanse of my hip once more, continuing to trail along my side, inside my sweater. The heat of his hand against my skin is as scorching as it was earlier.

"What are you doing to me?" He hums at my lips before moving his mouth to my jaw, then lowering for my neck.

"Me?" I choke as he nips near my collarbone.

His thigh presses harder. My legs spread wider.

"I only want to kiss you, and yet I want to touch you everywhere."

Please. Yes. Only, it feels important that we stick to kissing. Important to Brock.

So, I slide my hands over his biceps and into his hair, and I try to concentrate on his mouth and not the pulse in my pants. I try to hold still from rubbing my very needy core against his very firm thigh.

Brock must sense my resolve, and his hand goes no further than my side, but his thumb rubs at the underside of my breast. Teasing me. Tempting me.

We continue like this until Brock jumps off me once more. I remain on my back, panting and desperate, and clutching at my chest where my heart races within.

"Time," Brock strains, as if calling for a time-out, while he paces near the edge of the kitchen table. The room is dark except for the crackling flames and glow of the television. Although it's only midday, it might as well be midnight with the snowstorm swirling outside. Inside the fire is delightful, but the company is almost frightful. The sexual tension is more than I can bear.

Almost.

And still, we don't stop this game, going another round when London strikes midnight. Then, Cabo Verde Islands, a random collection of land in the Atlantic.

We hit a long pause, waiting for New York, which shares Eastern time with Michigan. Brock's promised roast beast is put on hold once more and we eat leftovers, clearing out the fridge, as if calling for a fresh start with the new year. We sit on the floor, propped up against the couch picnicking on our menagerie of foods.

However, as we near the call for midnight from New York, we're on the couch, making out like teenagers once more. Clothing remains on but askew. Brock has lost his shirt, and my sweater is pushed up just beneath my bra, allowing us skin to skin contact on our stomachs, and giving me the furnace that is Brock's flesh.

Hands roam but remain in the safety zones. Butts are grabbed. Bellies caressed. Backs clung to.

Brock's leg slips between my thighs once more as he lays on his back and I blanket him.

I've reached a breaking point and I'm ready to call time when the excitement on the television reaches my ears.

"Brock," I groan, wound too tight and almost ashamed by my lack of control. I need relief.

Sensing my frustration, Brock awkwardly rolls us on the couch, half his body over mine, his leg still between my thighs.

"Take it," Brock mutters to my mouth.

I groan, achy and weak. "You said only kissing."

"But you want to come." He nips at my lower lip. "You need it. And I want to see it. Hear it."

"What about you?" We've been kissing on and off for hours. I commend his stamina and appreciate his commitment to only connecting with our mouths, but I'm on the edge.

"Ten." The announcer on the television softly calls out as we lowered the volume at the start of this make out round.

"Take. It," Brock grits, grounding his leg harder against my throbbing center.

"Brock," I groan, frustrated and ready to retreat but his hand tightens on the back of my neck, the other hand cupping one butt cheek, holding me in place against him.

"Eight." I have no idea how I missed nine but when Brock tilts his hips and his stiff shaft jolts off center from my belly, I lose focus again.

"Gift it to me, then," Brock demands. As if taking an orgasm was too much to ask but gifting it to him will make it all the easier.

I moan at the increased pressure against my center, rocking my hips to create further friction.

"Six."

"I don't want to be selfish." We're no longer kissing but Brock still has his mouth on the side of my throat, nibbling at my skin and digging his fingertips into my backside.

"Be selfish," he commands, desperation sounding in his own strangled tone.

"But you—" I hiss at the next nudge of tension he creates, forcing me to roll my hips and brush harder against his leg.

"This is all for you."

"Four."

The countdown seems to spur him on, and Brock becomes hyper focused as his mouth comes to mine once more and his leg flexes against that sensitive spot on me. His hips insistently rock and I clutch at his lower back, silently begging him not to stop.

"Three."

"Yes," I whisper.

"Two."

"Oh, God," I croak.

"One."

Fireworks go off behind my eyelids before Brock demands I open them and I'm met with the heat of his coal-like eyes, flaming and bright, as I melt beneath him. Guilty but giddy.

That was incredible.

Draping my hand dramatically over my forehead, I shake my head, blinking back the glittery specks floating in the air over me.

"Happy New Year, snowflake." Brock grins with a mischievous glint to the teeth digging into his lower lip.

"Happy New Year, fireman. May it be your best year yet."

The added wish causes Brock to release his lower lip. His expression goes blank a second before he lowers and hovers just an inch from my lips.

"I call time until midnight hits Chicago."

"Oh God," I tiredly chuckle, until I read his face and realize he's serious.

This man wants to kiss me around the clock.

day 7

seven minutes swimming

January 1

chapter 11

[Brock]

Fuck, she is sexy. She not only let me *just* kiss her, she gave me that sweet orgasm around midnight and then continued the kissing game when Chicago struck twelve. By then we were both worn out. I'd made up for years' worth of useless kisses in a matter of hours, but I wanted more time with Pear.

My dick had never had such a workout, but I didn't want to rush like I'd said. I only wanted to savor every second our mouths connected. Of course, there was nibbling at her neck and feasting on her skin, but my hands didn't wander much other than outlining her serious curves and teasing the supple underside of her breasts.

There was no denying I wanted more of her, but I wanted to be given the gift, not just take from her.

When we finally agreed to call it a night, I escorted her to her room and went to mine but I didn't last more than three minutes before I was popping out of bed and knocking on her door.

Her tired groan was my permission to enter. "No more," she muttered into her pillow, hugging it tight beneath her head. I'd asked a lot of her today, but I still wanted to be close to her.

"Can I sleep with you?" I sounded like a child who'd had a bad dream. In many ways, I *was* that child deep down inside. A kid who'd given up his youth to help his family. A man who worked hard to provide for his family. A husband who lost his wife and struggled to keep up with his children. A firefighter who has possibly seen more than his share of trauma, and known death.

Without rolling from her side, Pear reached behind her and whipped the layers of blankets back to expose the sheet.

Shoving down my joggers, I slipped in behind her in only my boxer briefs and tugged her to me. The move was dangerous. She wasn't sleeping in anything more than tiny shorts, exposing her majestic thighs, while something skimpy covered her up top, offering more of her soft arms.

Still, I wrapped an arm over her middle, held her tight to my chest, and fell asleep within seconds.

Happy New Year indeed.

+++

When I wake alone, I'm not surprised, but easily hear Pear rustling around in the kitchen.

Sliding from her bed, I notice the wooden snowflake I made her on the nightstand. Smiling to myself, I reach for my sweats and slip into them, shivering from the temperature shift of her warm bed to the cold room. I return to my room for a shirt then wander into the kitchen.

"Good morning," I say, a little too cheerful, while hesitant. I don't want any regrets about yesterday.

"Happy New Year," She quickly glances at me without pausing from what she's hastily cooking on the stovetop. Corned beef hash sizzles. Eggs fry.

Wrapping my arms around her middle, I tug her back to my chest. She stiffens a second, but I hold on until she settles against me.

I kiss the side of her neck. "You okay today?"

"Yeah," she whispers, melting even more into me.

"You left the bed." I hum. The vanilla scent of her skin is intoxicating.

"We need to get going."

"Oh yeah?" I pull back and slip to her side, leaning my hip into the countertop. "What's today's plan?"

I should have asked for today to be my cheat day, but I'd been too excited yesterday morning when she suggested I take out the snowmobile. I haven't been snowmobiling in forever and sledding through the forest, a girl at my back, zipping along the trails, was amazing. It's been too long since I've been in the woods, and I'd forgotten how peaceful it can be. Living in Chicago, we have forest preserves, designated acres of woods with walking trails, but the space is not the same as the naked forest.

Today, however, is football day, although the championship of college bowl games doesn't take place for another week.

"Polar Plunge. We need to be there by ten."

"The what-what?" I blink. We have the tradition in Chicago, but I still don't think I've heard her correctly.

"Polar Plunge. It's a tradition. A cleansing of sorts. You rush into Lake Michigan, let the cold water cover you." She waves dramatically down her body. "The lake washes all the toxic negativity of last year out to sea and refreshes you for a new year."

"Excuse me?" This sounds like a load of modernistic horse crap.

"The Plunge is also a fundraiser for Special Olympics."

This is something I know, as the fire department is often on hand for the idiots running into the frigid lake in sub-zero temperatures. Even if it is a fundraiser, some people are just stupid about plunging. A minute tops is the recommendation. Fifteen minutes is the maximum before the body will shut down. Some people have to push the limits, sending their bodies into shock or hypothermia.

Personally, I don't want to dip my big toe into freezing lake water especially when the air temp outside is well below thirty-two degrees Fahrenheit. But here's what happens when you kiss an orgasm out of a girl, and she looks at you with sky blue eyes and kiss-swollen lips. You find yourself saying: "What should I wear?"

I don't have a bathing suit with me because there was no promise of pool-time at Cap's retreat. I don't even know if the camp has a pool and never considered we'd be dipping into a lake.

The smile that brightens Pear's face adds to my torture. "Your boxer briefs are fine."

No way. Everyone's going to see I have a boner for this woman, not to mention they will then witness my balls shriveling into frozen nuggets thanks to the cold lake.

But an hour later, I'm not the only guy making a fool of himself for someone else, or because of generosity and all that. Pear has already paid the online registration fee, making an additional charitable donation, and she refuses to tell me what she'd spent so I can reimburse her.

People stand around hopping from foot to foot, rubbing hands together and stroking up their arms to keep warm as we await a countdown.

There are two countdowns, actually. One for removing your clothes down to whatever you plan to submerge in and another count for the race to the lake.

When the clock starts ticking, I'm surprised how quickly people remove their winter jackets and I'm equally stunned by what they consider appropriate to wear into the lake. Plungers are in a variety of bikinis and speedos; some in board shorts and one-piece suits, while others are heading for the lake in wet suits and snorkeling gear like they'll be hanging out for a while. Still others have innertubes around their waists. One guy is wearing a clown outfit.

So I finally understand when Pear repeatedly reassured me no one would be looking at me in my black boxer briefs.

"Other than to maybe check out what you're packing," she'd teased when we pulled up and parked in the public lot, which was overflowing with other fools like us.

As for Pear, she's in a bright red one-piece suit, like a lifeguard might wear and my *yank*-bank is full to overflowing of fantasies of what I want to do to her.

As the countdown starts for the race to the water, Pear takes my hand, squeezing it tight, and I glance down at our fingers locked together. Gazing back up at her, her eyes gleam and she gives me a teasing grimace.

Fuck, do I like this woman.

When the pop of a confetti gun goes off, Pear starts shrieking and runs toward the lake, tugging at my hand.

"Fuck," I holler, as others cry out as well at the first connection with the icy lake. The lake is actually warmer than the air, but it makes no difference. Forty-degrees or four, the fresh water is fucking freezing.

Still, I follow Pear thigh deep. We've been warned not to submerge our heads. Pear drops my hand, sucks in a large breath and holds, grits her teeth, and drops below the surface up to her shoulders. Like a graceful swan taking off from the water, she shoots upright and lets out a delighted scream before scrubbing at her face. Her pale skin pebbles. That red one-piece is seersuckers to her body, outlining the contours of her curves. Her nipples are erect and poking at the tight material like they could cut through the fabric. She's as luscious as a ripe pear, and I want to take a huge bite of her.

Instead, I follow suit and drop below the surface to my shoulders before slowly standing to my full height again. Pear is shivering, clutching her arms in front of her chest, and I reach for her wrists and tug her to me. She stumbles in the cold water but when my mouth crashes against hers, I suddenly don't feel the chill. The heat of her mouth is one thing, but Pear kisses me like she wants to devour me. Like she wants to pull me into her soul and keep me there.

Her eagerness is as refreshing as this frigid bath, cleansing me of the negativity of past relationships and opening my lungs to fresh air. I feel like I can breathe for the first time in a long while. Maybe my heart is open as well, to the potential of a new status.

Taken.

By this pear of a woman, trembling in the cold lake while clinging to me with her warm mouth and hot-as-sin body.

"Done?" I ask, pulling back and tipping my head to hers. Her lips are red, her eyes bright blue.

She nods, tucking her arms tighter to her chest, to cover her breasts and the hard nips protruding against her suit. I duck and clasp her around the back of her legs, hitching her up and over my shoulder in a fireman's hold.

Pear squeals again, slapping my ass once before tucking her thumbs into the waistband of my boxer briefs as a means to hold onto something.

"Careful there. Don't want everyone to see the good side of me."

"And your backside is the good side?" she grunts as I carry her over my shoulder.

"Had enough people tell me to kiss their ass."

"That would mean their ass was good, not yours." Pear huffs.

"Semantics. My ass. Their ass." I turn my head and nip at her leg, just below her ass.

Her retaliation is pinching mine.

I set Pear down on a blanket covering the cool sand. We both do an awkward dance of rubbing off the water with towels and trying to redress with shaky limbs. The recommendation is to immediately change out of the wet clothing and the public bathroom is open for such a thing. There is a celebration for all who took the plunge, but Pear suggests we return to my truck.

"I just wanted to do the Plunge. Support Special Olympics." She shrugs, glancing down at her lap once we are inside the cab. A towel covers her lower body. She's wearing her winter jacket zipped up to her neck and her boots, minus pants. The seat warmers are on; the heat is set to full blast.

"I wanted to symbolically wash away any lingering negative aura."

I'm curious what toxins she feels still waffle around her. "Like what?"

Lifting her head, she absentmindedly stares out the windshield at the beach dotted with people in various states of changing their clothes and toasting to one another.

"Reggie, mainly. The financial mess. I guess I just saw this moment as closure." She finally looks at me. "Or a baptism."

"That's rather deep," I tease but instantly regret the joke. Swallowing hard, I add, "I get it, though. That did feel good." I nod toward the lake. "I feel different."

However, a seven-minute dip in the lake isn't the only thing that's made a change. It's been seven *days* with this woman. One full week has made me feel better about myself.

She didn't judge me when I worked on the dressers but encouraged me to fix them. Hell, she even had me building owl boxes, which was a good start to constructing furniture. And she appreciated the wooden snowflake I made her.

She didn't scold me for making a mess when I canned pears, but simply helped me clean up, like she helped me with the fence posts, at first.

She let me have my fun with the snowmobile, going along for the ride even when she was nervous, and she wasn't upset when I couldn't complete a project, like sanding the runners on that old sleigh.

She'd been easy going at every turn and obstacle, and then good-natured and open-minded on the straight run, like kissing her all afternoon and night yesterday.

Like skiing down a black diamond, there'd been a risk, a vulnerability, but the rush had been worth every second our mouths connected.

When Pear remains silent, I reverse the truck out of the parking lot.

She shivers beside me, and she should have taken off her wet suit instead of wrapping up in a towel and tugging on her winter coat. With her feet in her boots and her bare legs trembling, she looks ridiculous but adorable.

Once we return to the house, she enters the front door but stops to open a closet just inside the small entryway. I hear the distinct flip of a switch.

"Shower." I'm not taking no for an answer. She needs to get out of that suit and into warm clothes but first she needs to heat up her entire body.

"I have a better idea." Turning toward me, she drops her winter coat and the wet towel at her waist. "Let's hot tub."

+ + +

I don't know how I missed the tub other than it is tucked against the house in a corner and not easily seen from the back window which was shielded by the Christmas tree until only a day ago. Yesterday, we'd been busy during the wintery storm and before that I hadn't had any need to circle around to the back of the house. The entire orchard was their backyard.

Shoved up against the house with a privacy screen on one side, the hot tub is bubbling and steaming in the cold January First air when Pear and I gingerly step into the liquid heaven and lower to our shoulders. She brought fresh towels outside with us, along with two lightweight blankets for added warmth once we are done.

For now, I only want to concentrate on the bubbles boiling around me and the jet stream pulsing against my lower back.

I sigh, closing my eyes and tipping back my head on the edge of the tub. "How did I not know about this?"

Pear laughs, but I don't open my eyes, too entranced by how amazing the water feels.

"Dad added it a few years back. I imagine he likes to come out here at night and watch the stars light the sky."

My eyes open. Another gloomy sky hangs overhead this morning and yet a day has never looked so bright, so promising. My gaze falls to Pear. She's my promise.

We smile at one another, keeping silent with our thoughts, and relishing in the relaxation of the tub, but as I naturally run hot, it doesn't take long before the bubbling pool is too much for me.

I slip up to the edge of the tub, dangling my feet in the water.

"Hot?" Pear questions.

The corner of my mouth curls upward as she knows the answer.

"Yes, you are." Her eyes trail down my body and I laugh. Her gaze certainly makes a man feel wanted.

While we haven't seen one another naked, Pear in that suit has left little to the imagination.

Her gaze stalls on my abs. A trail of hair runs below my belly button and vanishes into my boxer briefs. I'm not into making it all disappear down there but I do keep it well-groomed.

Pear crosses the small pool in one easy stroke before popping up between my spread knees. I lean back on my arms and watch as her hands cover my thighs, spreading my legs wider apart.

"It's so unfair," she whispers appreciatively, swiping one finger down my midsection, starting at my chest and bumping down my belly like a skier on moguls. When she reaches my waistband, she teasingly drags her fingertip back and forth against the thick band. "I was selfish last night."

"Yeah, you were," I tease, causing her head to shoot upright. "And I want you to be selfish with me again."

Her fingers wrap around the waist of my underwear, and she tugs. Instantly, I catch her wrist with one of my hands.

"What are you doing?" My voice is rough, my mouth suddenly dry.

"Being selfish," she hums as her gaze lowers to the stiffness growing in my boxer briefs.

"How is *that* being selfish?"

"I want to taste you."

Fuuuck! "I—" Admitting that's it has been a while since someone went down on me would be embarrassing. I just haven't had the same desire I once had to meet a random woman in a bar and hook up for one night only. The guys at the firehouse would crudely joke lack of sex has been my problem lately. They have no idea how close they are to the truth.

"I'm clean," I tell her, wanting her to know to some extent my sexual history. "Went to the doctor in November. Go every year around my birthday." And it's been eight months since I've had sex.

"I don't think I'll last very long," I add.

She's looking up at me with wide eyes and pouty lips. She isn't even intentionally playing sex kitten and that makes me want to purr.

Releasing her wrist, I lean back again and hitch up my hips so she can lower my boxer briefs to my ankles before she tosses them behind her, letting them float away in the tub. The cool edge of the tub is a shock at first but when she tenderly kisses my tip, all thoughts of the temperature are gone. My focus is solely on the woman between my knees, looking up at me with hesitant eyes while pressing her lips to my lower head.

"Snowflake," I groan. I'm as stiff as an icicle but as hot as a flame when she wraps her hand around my dick and tugs upward while dropping her mouth around the head.

"You're so big."

Words every man wants to hear.

"Jesus." *Mary and Joseph, and all the holy saints*. My eyes roll back, and my hips jolt as Pear smooths her mouth down my length, slowly drawing me to the back of her throat.

"Oh baby," I whimper like a lost child. I lift a hand and stroke over her head, combing my fingers through her damp hair.

Pear drags back up my shaft, swirls her tongue around the crown, and then opens wide and takes me in again.

"Ffff—" I can't even form a complete word as she hollows her cheeks and slips up and down, gliding me in and out of her wet mouth. Her hand pumps the base, working what she can't take deep between her sexy lips. And I'm a mess when she cups my balls with her other palm.

My hips jut upward, and Pear chokes. "Sorry. *Sorry*. But *please* don't stop."

She shakes her head while keeping her concentration on the task in her hand, and in her mouth.

I'm totally going to blow too quick because she's too good. Her mouth is too warm. Her hand the right pressure. Her tongue doing that thing and—

"Paradise." Cupping her cheeks and attempting to tug her free is the only warning I can give her, but she clamps down harder, sucking stronger, and I go off like the fireworks last night celebrating a new year. Little stars dance before my eyes, as I pet her hair, and she swallows down the raining explosion before dragging up my length and pressing a final kiss to the tip.

Her head slowly lifts. Her lips still cherry-red but damp. Her eyes are bright and wide when she says, "You called me Paradise."

"Because you are fucking heaven, baby."

chapter 12

[Pear]

I could quip that I've heard that statement before but in Brock's strained tone, it isn't a line. Spoken with pure reverence despite the profanity, his eyes are the thing that further confirm his sincerity. That coal-color is a soft black, like liquid ink, and I want him to scribble all over me.

I want him to call me Paradise and tell me I'm perfect, like he did last night.

Instead, he moves forward, forcing me back, and dips back into the hot tub, retrieving his boxer briefs and pulling them up his legs to cover himself.

Suddenly, his hands are on my hips, and he pulls me up and out of the water, setting me on the edge of the tub.

Paybacks is on the tip of my tongue but as Brock scans my body from the top of my head to my knees as my lower legs remain in the heated pool, I can't speak. I'm not certain a man has ever looked at me the way he's admiring me.

"Breast guy or ass man?" I finally ask, as I anxiously await his move. He isn't touching me. He isn't stroking my legs or standing to kiss me. Instead, he's visually exploring every slope and curve of my body.

This one-piece suit, cut straight across my chest in a bandeau style, leaves little to the imagination. My breasts aren't that big for being a bigger girl. My belly is flat but still soft. My thighs are thick and my—

"Hips," he says, drawing my attention back to his eyes. "I'm a hips man."

He reaches for mine, tugging me to the edge of the lip around the tub. My knees automatically spread, allowing his broad shoulders to slip between them. He slowly stands, running his hands over my hips before gliding up my sides similar to the way he touched me last night, when his palms skimmed underneath my sweater. He didn't even touch my breasts, as if content to play with the underside, and tease the hell out of me with the thick pad of his thumb.

"My breasts are small," I say next, nervous and hating myself for pointing out a fault.

"A mouthful." He licks his lips but doesn't lower for one. "And do not criticize yourself." His tone sharpens like when I thought he was making a fat girl joke or when I told him what Reggie said.

But Reggie has no place here.

Only Brock. Between my thighs. With his palms stroking my sides.

His sudden movement startles me. His hands clap onto my inner thighs and spread me wider.

"I want to see every inch of you and yet there is something enticing about this bathing suit covering up all the good parts."

He makes no move to remove my suit, instead lowering his head to set his mouth around my covered breast, then nip me through the material. "Mouthful. Perfection."

A smile fills his voice as he slides his hands back to my hips and moves his chest closer to my center. A pulsing beat strikes like a marching band, drumming against a sensitive spot. My legs tremble and I want to clamp them together, needing friction for the sweet spot.

Brock does not disappoint, as he smooths his hand over my belly and lowers his thumb to strum over my covered core. He presses forward, watching as my wet suit molds to every fold down there. Holding his hand firmly on my lower belly, he swirls his thumb in the most delicious circles, and I tip back my head, catching myself with my arms extended outward on the pool's edge.

"That feels so good."

"You feel good," he counters, adding more pressure, building the tension. My legs begin to wobble, and my knees bounce. Brock scoops up one of my legs and hitches it over his shoulder to stabilize me.

"I want my lips and tongue on you, in you, tasting every last drop I wring from this sweet pussy."

Holy Christmas stockings. I cannot remember the last time someone did such a thing.

"You don't need to do that," I hum, enthralled by what he is doing to me with that powerful thumb.

However, Brock stills, forcing me to lift my head and meet his eyes. He doesn't ask and I'm glad not to tell. My ex didn't like the act and that's just too embarrassing to admit.

When his eyes narrowed, his voice is rough and tight. "You're a woman who deserves to be eaten. Savored. Devoured."

"Good words," I mutter about his multiple suggestions, but Brock isn't joking around.

My suit is tugged to the side and his tongue swipes up my center so fast I almost fall backward with the shock. Then he's forcing my knees wide enough each touches the edge of the hot tub, and his lips are kissing me down there like he takes my mouth. Hungry. Eager. Honest.

I know how Brock eats legitimate meals—fast and rushed. However, he's not so quick to finish here, and the time he takes to outline every fold with the tip of his tongue and slick through every crease has me a trembling mess in minutes. With my fingers in his hair, clutching at his head, my hips have a will of their own, dancing against his mouth in a rhythm without metrics.

"Brock," I choke out, digging my fingers tighter into his hair. I slide my hands to the back of his neck, holding him in place. Selfish.

But I want him. I want *this* for more than a twelve-day sentence. I want twelve months. A dozen years. Twelve times twelve times. Just more.

And my body goes off as the silly chant repeats in my head.

Twelve times twelve times twelve times, like the rapid beating of my heart and the flashing of midnight. The end of a day. The start of a new year.

This man is my polar plunge. My refresher and I am totally spent as I wind down the spiral he's spun me on.

Slowly, I release his hair, and he draws back, brushing his lips against the insides of my thighs.

"Fireman." I swallow hard around the nickname.

He chuckles. "You say that like I'm Spiderman or a goddamn superhero."

Cupping his cheeks and leaning forward while he rights my suit, I stare directly into his eyes.

"That's because putting out fires and saving people's lives makes you a superhero. To me."

chapter 13

[Brock]

Fuck. She can't mean it, and I kiss her mouth to distract myself from how the word sounds in my head.

Superhero.

We kiss for a few minutes more before I break free and pull her hands from my face. Her fingertips are shriveled.

"I'm waterlogged," I admit. "And you're becoming a raisin."

Pear giggles, leans forward to kiss me one more time, and then hikes her legs over the side of the hot tub. She rushes for a towel and then adds a blanket around herself while I step out of the tub as well. I'm surprised I'm not as cold as I expected, and glance up to find a heating lamp on in the overhang above us.

Note to self: turn that off as it's a fire hazard if left unattended.

I don't need to worry as Pear flips that magical switch once we enter the house and I demand she shower first.

"I want to call my kids anyway."

Today marks a new year, and while the day isn't very exciting, as far as holidays go, being that most people celebrated last night, I still want to check in with them. I'd spoken with them the day I arrived, but they were too wrapped up in the excitement of their mother's wedding to give me more than five minutes on the phone.

Pear understands and I head to Cap's room when she enters the bathroom.

"Dad?" Nick answers on the second ring.

"Hey, Nicky."

"Dad," he drones tightly.

I'm not allowed to call him Nicky anymore. Nick. He started going by the short, sharp name in high school, but six years later I'm still struggling *not* to call him by the nickname.

"Hi. Happy New Year."

"Happy New Year. I didn't expect to hear from you."

"Are you busy?" I ask, staring down at my lap. I removed both the wet towel and my drenched boxer briefs, opting for the throw blanket around my belly to keep me warm until it's my turn for the shower.

"Nah. I'm putting you on speaker phone. Ellie is here."

"Hey, baby," I address my girl, finding my throat thickening for some reason.

"Hi, Daddy." Eighteen-years old and she still calls me daddy sometimes. That lump in my throat becomes a heavy rock. "We didn't think you'd be able to call us from the probation camp."

"Restorative justice," I correct. For some reason, I don't explain my current situation. Instead, I quip, "But I was given time off for good behavior."

Ellie giggles. Nick remains silent.

"How was the wedding?" The rock clogging my throat drops to a boulder in my belly. I don't really want to know about my ex-wife and my best friend's nuptials, but I'm trying to be polite.

A moment of silence passes, and I can almost envision my kids sharing a glance, deciding how to answer me. I'm opening my mouth, prepared to say it doesn't matter, when Nick replies.

"Mom looked beautiful. Kenny, too."

"I bet." Melissa was always a beautiful woman. I'd never paid attention to Kenny's appearance. She was one of the guys. My best friend. I didn't see her in any way other than a nice-looking woman but not someone I was attracted to. Apparently, Melissa found her attractive, though.

"You guys don't happen to have a picture of the two of you together, do you?" I hold my breath, knowing my kids both stood up in the small ceremony. In a flash, a text message pops up in the header of my phone.

"Just sent one," Nick adds.

I click over to the text app and enlarge the shared photo. "Damn, buddy. You clean up nice," I tease while my vision blurs.

My kids are so fucking grown up. Nick might be twenty-one and still have a baby-ish face, but his body is all man and we've had plenty of discussions about how the machine he is belongs on the field and nowhere else. No bar fights. No aggression toward women.

My baby girl, on the other hand, has looked like a woman for years, and she's stunning in a deep red gown.

"Ellie, it probably wasn't fair for you to outshine the brides, sweetheart. You look gorgeous." Her brown hair has golden highlights, and it's swept up in some elaborate hairstyle.

"Thanks, Dad."

"So, what are you guys doing today? What have you been up to?"

"Kenny wanted us to come over."

Mentally, I protest that Kenny and Melissa get more time with my kids. I'm missing out on two weeks with this twelve-day gig, and I brought it up to Cap, who brushed me off, knowing the kids would only be gone the week of Christmas for the wedding. Nick and Ellie are both home for a month between their semester breaks.

"I thought they were going on a honeymoon."

"They leave tomorrow," Ellie explains. "But we're home now." *Home*, meaning my house.

Silence fills the line again.

"Actually—" Ellie's voice begins but some kind of struggle ensues and what sounds like the phone hitting the floor clambers through mine.

"You guys okay?"

A minute passes before Nick responds. "Yeah, we just—"

"We're having a party, Daddy." Ellie hollers as if feet away from the phone.

"Ellie," Nick groans.

"What?" I chuckle, not half as upset as maybe I should be.

"We each asked five friends to come over," Ellie explains. "I promise we'll clean up everything."

"Guys," I groan, lowering my head and squeezing at my forehead. A party at my house without me present is the last thing I need.

"We're ordering pizzas and watching the big game," Nick adds.

"No alcohol," I demand, but Nick is twenty-one.

"Dad," he groans.

"Ellie." My girl is a good girl, and Nick's friends have all been warned away from her by him, being the protective, big brother he is. But alcohol and college kids aren't a great mix. Not that I have any say when they are away at school, but I'm not liking this combination in my home.

For some reason, Pear's voice whispers through my head, reminding me I need to let my kids make their own choices, and their own mistakes. Doesn't mean I don't want to prevent something dangerous or harmful from happening to them, but they're still good kids. Nick will watch out for Ellie. And Ellie can hold her own against his friends.

"Okay." I sigh.

"What?" Ellie squeaks.

"Ow," Nick grunts.

"What happened?"

"Ellie hit me." The fake pout in Nick's voice suggests he isn't really hurt.

I chuckle.

"She said you'd let us have the party if we only asked," Nick explains.

Have I been so tough on my kid that he's too afraid to ask if he can have friends over? For that fact . . . is he preferring I'm *not* home, so I don't embarrass him? These are hard thoughts to have.

"Nick." I swallow that lump rising back up in my throat. "I trust you."

Silence fills the line again, and I'm assuming another eyeball conversation is happening between siblings.

"Gone by midnight," I suggest.

"Sure, Dad." Nick's voice sounds lighter.

"But no drinking and driving. If people need to stay the night, just . . . let me know." I should definitely know who is staying at my house when I'm not present.

"Absolutely," Ellie confirms.

"Okay, well, have fun." I swallow hard once more, wishing I was the one ordering pizza and watching the game with my kids. But I also understand that hanging with their old man isn't high on the list of good times anymore.

"I love you guys." My nose starts to tickle. My eyes burn.

"Love you, too, Daddy," Ellie says, her voice cheerful and sweet as always.

"Love you." Nick's voice is quick but not insincere. He's a good boy. A good man. I have much to be thankful for with my kids.

On that note, the phone goes dead, and I stare down at the device in my hands. After a quick text to Ma in the family group chat with her and my siblings, I have one more text to send.

I open the contact labeled Nat's Parents, type a message and hit send.

Happy New Year. Thinking of you.

I don't expect a reply. I rarely get one.

A short knock comes to Cap's bedroom door, and I lift my head as Pear opens it, hesitating as she pokes her head around the barrier.

"Hey. I'm done in the shower. You're up." A smile fills her rosy face, freshly scrubbed and sparkling a bit with light makeup. Her lips are brighter red. Her lashes darker.

"You okay?" she questions, opening the door wider.

"Yeah." I blink once and rub my eyes with my forefinger and thumb. "Just checking in with my kids."

The tender touch of Pear's hand on my arm has me flinching. My eyes snap open to see her pulling back her hand.

She remains quiet and I lift my phone, giving it a gentle shake as I stare back at the device. "I sent a text to my family, and one to . . ." My throat tightens. "One to Nat's parents."

Pear doesn't ask at first and quiet seconds pass between us before she says, "Who is Nat?"

"Was. He was a newbie in the department under my charge." I twist my lips. With a deep inhale and a shuddering exhale, I add. "He passed away a few years ago."

Without looking up at Pear, I explain. "It was my fault."

"What? No. *No,*" her quiet plea softens. Her lowers beside me on the edge of the bed and wraps her hand around my forearm.

"Bomb threat. Turned into a three-alarm fire." I almost can't breathe as I recall the smoke, the heat, and the scream. "He fell down an airshaft. Four floors."

Closing my eyes, I add, "He was only twenty-four." He had so much life before him. No wife. No kids. Just a happy-go-lucky guy with a laugh like a hyena. He was so fucking funny.

"Brock, that was not your fault."

"I trained him," I snap at her, lifting my head and glaring at her before lowering my gaze once more.

Pear goes quiet and I turn the phone over and over in my hands. Her hand slips from my forearm, my skin suddenly cold without her touch.

"Have you spoken with someone about this? About how you feel?"

On the tip of my tongue is a retort. Telling her once again I don't need a shrink. But I remember what she said. She wanted to grow bigger.

"Had mandatory sessions. Ten of them. There was nothing to discuss." The therapist didn't think I was making progress, and she could have kept me from returning to work, but I explained to Cap that I was fine. Risks came with the job. I understood that I had nothing to do with Nat's misstep or the hidden shaft. Still, guilt ate at me.

"But . . ." I draw out a heavy breath. "It's one reason I don't want Nick joining the department."

I don't want to lose my son like Nat's parents lost him. I'd never be able to forgive myself. I wouldn't know how to go on without my boy.

Eventually, Pear asks. "Do you want to talk about it?"

I didn't. I really didn't, so I shake my head. "I just want to shower."

Pear's voice remains quiet. "All yours."

I shouldn't have snapped at her. And I should have told her more. Maybe I should talk to someone. Just not today.

I stand instead, and head to the bathroom needing a few minutes to be alone and clear my head.

+ + +

"What's all this?" A chuckle fills my voice. I feel better after my shower. I feel even lighter because Nat's parents responded to my text with wishes for a happy new year. In my heart, I know they never blamed me. I'd put the fault on myself.

However, I didn't want to think about Nat right now. Not with the spread set up on the kitchen table. While I'd asked my question, I can see for myself that Pear has been busy. Chili in a slow cooker. Chips and topping options in small bowls around the cooker. Cheese and crackers on a fancy board; pear slices among them. The timer on the oven beeps and Pear removes a baking sheet of cookies.

"How did you do all this?" I didn't think I'd been in the shower that long, but apparently, she's a kitchen wizard.

"The chili won't be ready for a bit, but the other stuff was in the fridge. The cookie dough is the pre-made kind I found in the freezer. Not my best cookies, but they work."

I glance up at her and notice she's wearing a bright red sweater and hip-hugging jeans. I haven't seen her in such an outfit yet.

"You're dressed in color."

Pear glances down at herself.

"I've only seen you in a variety of whites." And a red bathing suit earlier today.

I've killed the vibe with my memories of Nat.

"Oh." Pear swipes a hand self-consciously over her stomach. "I used to wear a lot of black. Like *a lot*. And when I finally moved on from Reggie, I made a major wardrobe change. White is so much brighter. But . . ." She laughs. "I do own other colors. Like red." She plucks at her sweater.

I smile but her smile in return is weak.

"This is quite a spread for lunch."

Pear shrugs. "Well, it's game day."

Right, college football. I glance back at her sweater. "Please tell me you are not—"

"Go Bulldogs." She timidly raises a fist in solidarity with University of Georgia.

I want to punch myself in the face for her sudden cautious actions. This *is* my fault, and I step closer to her.

"You know, you and me cannot be an us if you root for red. I'm a blue and gold man. Go Wolverines." Lifting my hand, I brush back a long, dark strand of her hair which is so soft and shiny. Her vanilla scent tickles my nose, and I want to restore us to how we were earlier.

"Time," I whisper.

"Time for what?"

Leaning toward her, I hover over her mouth. My gaze seeks her eyes, hoping she'll take my meaning.

When she doesn't close the distance, I accept that I need to ask for what I want. "Kiss me."

Pear leans forward and our mouths meet but the kiss is too quick and stiff.

Nope. Not having this. "I'm sorry I snapped," I say as I pull back. "That's on me. Nat is a difficult subject."

"And you should really talk to someone about him."

"I—" My rejection of the idea cuts off when she lifts those blue eyes to me. Eyes the color of a cold lake that was meant to cleanse me of any negativity. "I'll think about it."

"Really?" Her brows lift. Her eyes widen.

"Yes." I'm not just blowing a promise at her, either. "I'll look into something when I get home. For now, I'm serving my twelve-day . . . service."

"Service?" Pear snorts, but the sound is more humor than sarcasm. "You should be servicing me, then."

I grin, tipping up a brow, before Pear blushes and recants. "I meant serve. You should be serving me." She waves at the spread on the table.

"I will. Take a seat. I'll bring over the cheese board and a glass of wine." I arch a brow to confirm that's what she'd like.

"That sounds perfect."

Reaching for her hair again, I scoop pieces behind her ear. "You're perfect, baby."

day 8

eight cows need milkin'

January 2

chapter 14

[Pear]

Brock was not expecting my enthusiasm for a football game, and his surprise shows when I pull out a deck of battered old cards.

"Let's play a game."

"Now?" he questions.

"Pick two cards. And I'll pick two cards."

He peers skeptically at me but tugs two from the fanned deck in my hands. While he waits patiently, I draw two.

"Okay, we can share our cards with each other." I show him I have the seven of spades and the three of diamonds.

He has the eight of clubs and the queen of hearts.

"At the end of the first quarter, if the score is seven to three or anything ending in seven or three, I win. And if the score is eight to twelve, or anything ending in eight with a twelve, you win."

Brock scoffs. "For my team or yours?" He's still shocked I'm a Georgia fan while he's all Michigan.

"Either team."

"And what do I win?" He reaches forward and tugs at my hips as I stand in front of where he sits on the couch.

"Well, when I was a kid and we played this game, the payout was a quarter. At the end of a game, you might have won a dollar. But I think we can wager something more substantial." I smile slowly.

Brock's eyes spark. "Hmm, I could think of a few things."

The fog surrounding him after his tale about Nate has dissipated. I wish he didn't feel so responsible for something beyond his control. He couldn't have predicted a hidden air shaft. However, Brock is a man who does not take his responsibilities lightly. He also needs help processing what happened, even if it was years ago.

I'm slowly realizing that it isn't that Brock doesn't feel his emotions, it's that he feels everything so much. He tries to shut off the difficult sections of his life, like an out-of-control fire hydrant. Self-preservation is his stronghold.

"We'll pick new cards each quarter."

"So just to clarify, when I win at the end of the first quarter, I can have anything I want." Confident and cocky, his voice drops. How the score will end in an eight and twelve in one quarter is beyond me but best of luck to him.

"Anything. And if I win, I get anything I ask."

Brock squeezes my hips, jostling me a little bit. "Going down on you again is going to be a win for me as well, snowflake."

"Oh, we talkin' sexual payouts?" I tease, hoping we were, but I have a bigger favor to ask.

"If you play your cards right . . ." he counters.

We both laugh. The tension snapped for now.

At the end of the first quarter, however, I win and have my first ask. "I want you to promise you'll go to therapy. Not just say you'll think about it." I recognize a vague vow when I hear it.

Brock's mouth pops open. Then shuts. "This isn't how I saw this game going."

Maybe now isn't the time for the suggestion but . . . "You assured me I could ask for anything. And I want to trust your word."

We stare at one another for a long hard minute while commercials about chips and beer play on the television.

"You can trust me," he strongly states. "But I still thought you'd ask for an orgasm."

I chuckle. "Maybe when I win next quarter. But your mental health is more important to me, Brock."

He stares at me, until I'm so uncomfortable I'm almost ready to tell him to forget I asked. I'd take the orgasm, but with *my* current mindset, relaxing into something so selfish would be difficult.

"Fine." His reply is sharp, resolved, but also strangely decisive.

"Promise?"

"I swear."

"Pinky promise," I tease.

"I have something better than wrapping our fingers together." With that, I'm falling backward on the couch and victory is mine when his fingers do indeed connect with another part of me.

By the time the Bulldogs finally win the game, I've had four orgasms. And one promissory note.

A new team record.

Go, me.

+ + +

"What's going on?" Brock asks in the morning as he shuffles into the kitchen while I'm hanging up the landline phone on the wall.

He looks a little rough this morning as he scratches beneath his chin. His hair is sticking up on one side. Just looking at that silvery blend on his jaw has me clenching my thighs together. His mouth was sweet last night but the way he'd rubbed that beard against my skin . . . I shiver. A good shiver.

Last night, we slept in the same bed again with him curled around me. We'd done all our kissing and canoodling on the couch. The bed was strictly for sleeping.

"Mr. Renshaw's cows need milking."

"Excuse me?" Brock's brows lift.

"Mr. Renshaw is the farmer whose property butts up to Dad's. His cows are the ones that wander into the orchard sometimes. He called because something happened to his milking machine. Power out or generator down." I wave a hand. "Anyway, he needs help and I guess Dad typically steps up."

Brock eyes me suspiciously. "But your dad isn't here."

"Nope. We are, so he's getting two for the price of one."

"I don't know anything about milking cows, snowflake," Brock counters, dropping his hand.

"Neither do I, but he needs us."

"I am not fondling some cow's tits."

"Good thing they are called teats."

"I'm not squeezing its nipples." His gaze drops to my chest where he fondled and squeezed mine last night but milking a cow will not be the same thing.

"Afraid you'll get turned on?" I tease.

"No. Because I was already hard." He grabs himself. "But now I'm not."

I pout. "Someone is grouchy today." When we played our card game last night, he refused to let me touch him as one of my quarter wins. Maybe he needs a little something to right him getting up on the wrong side of the bed this morning.

He huffs and turns his head toward the coffee machine. "Is there coffee?"

"Fireman," I whisper and watch as his eyes close. He takes a deep breath before his shoulders relax.

"Just let me have a cup of coffee and we can go."

While Brock crosses the kitchen, I rapidly clap my hands together and bounce up and down on my toes. "I love you."

Brock and I both freeze. Him with his hand reaching for a mug. Me with a gasp and my hands clasped beneath my chin.

"I mean . . . You know . . . I love you as in I love that you're doing this. For the cows." My face heats with embarrassment and I cringe, aware of my faux pas.

Brock keeps his back to me as he pours himself a cup of coffee and I want to melt into the hardwood floor at saying something so stupid.

Falling in love is not on the twelve-day list.

He spins with his mug in hand, then leans back against the counter while lifting the steaming cup to his lips.

"For the cows," he repeats, watching me over the rim of his mug. "Because nothing says love like cows."

"Like jars of pears. And owls."

"We're at Valentine's cows now, are we?" His bushy brow hitches.

"Official animal."

"I thought the owls were."

"Those are birds," I counter, still horrified that I said I loved him, even if I meant it in a playful, noncommittal, I won kind of way.

"Ah. I'm learning so much about romance. Best to be prepared for the next holiday."

"The twelve days of Valentine's?" I shrug my shoulders, attempting to keep things light and hope my mishap disappears into the snowy abyss.

"Now *that* holiday is more than a day?" He chuckles. "I can't keep up. Maybe it should be the *fourteen* days of Valentine's."

"That's a lot of love-gifting." However, is it any different than the twelve days of gifts from a true love at Christmas?

Brock continues to watch me while sipping his coffee. When he lowers his cup, his gaze never leaves my face.

"Might be worth the challenge."

I chew on my lower lip. Does he mean me? I'm the challenge. Or does he mean fourteen days in another month would be a challenge? Like the twelve days he'll have put in here at the farm. Has it been difficult to be here?

I hate the unwarranted doubt. Brock has taken each task I've given, mostly without complaint, and completed them. The fact our little forced proximity has turned into more hasn't seemed to bother him one bit, either. But what happens when these twelve days are complete?

Would Valentine's Day mean anything for either of us?

Would we both be alone again, like we were at the start of his sentence?

There are things I need to tell him.

I don't want to go back to being alone.

I don't want to go back to living without him.

Selfish.

"Snowflake," Brock calls, and I blink, knowing I zoned out. "You okay?"

"Yeah," I lie. "Just excited to milk some cows."

chapter 15

[Brock]

My heart should not have grown three sizes in my chest at her declaration.

I love you.

She didn't mean me directly. She meant it in that off-handed way one says it, like when Ellie was little, and I'd come home with ice cream cones as a treat.

I love you. For ice cream.

And now cows? I snort. *Way to try to dig out of that pile of snow, Pear.*

Still, my chest seized, and I held my breath, inhaling false hope that she might mean the words. Like she might say them again and there would be honest emotion behind them that has nothing to do with livestock. And everything to do with me.

What a fucking idiot I am.

I'm equally stupid for giving in to sitting on a wooden stool that feels like it's going to collapse underneath my weight and grab the *teats* of a cow.

"Just start at the top and give a squeeze. Don't be afraid you'll hurt her. She's a mother. She's tough." Mr. Renshaw is exactly what one might expect in an older gent who has spent most of his life in a variety of seasons. His skin is weathered by the elements of extreme cold and blistering sunshine. Pride fills his face as well as gratitude as roughly a dozen or so people have showed up to help him milk his precious cows.

I'd offered to look at his machine or his generator in hopes that I could be of mechanical use instead of manual labor. Manual, as in, physically wrapping my hand around a cow's distended nipple and milking it. However, Mr. Renshaw declined the offer. A repairman was on the way, but the cows could not wait.

"Don't be afraid to give her a nudge, too. A gentle head butting never hurt." He points to where another man has his head leaning into the side of a cow to keep her in place.

Personally, I want to bang my head on the side of this barn.

Then I look over at Pear whose smile is so wide, like she's ready to lasso one of these beasts and take it home like a lap dog. For a woman who has lived in large cities most of her life, she's embracing her inner farm-girl and loving this moment.

I'm also reminded of how she wistfully adored the antique sleigh in her dad's barn. The job was too big for me to complete in one day; the project too extensive. Guilt strikes. I didn't want to disappoint her.

Turning back to the task at hand, I mentally gripe. *Okay, Brock. You can do this. It's like jacking off.*

Only, it wasn't. And I had to get that thought out of my head or I'd never be able to do the deed again. I'd need to be able to complete the one-handed talent in the future because Pear had given me years-worth of mental fantasies to replay on repeat.

Her body is my catnip. Her hips. Her scent. The sounds she made when my mouth was on her. I couldn't seem to get enough. Kissing her was heaven. Touching her was out of this world.

I wanted to keep her, but I didn't know how.

We joked a lot about Valentine's Day. The future date feels so far away and yet my twelve-day sentence has passed too quickly. I have less than four days left at her dad's farm. Then what? We say goodbye and go our separate ways. I didn't like that idea. Not one bit.

"How's it going there, Farmer Brock?" Pear's sweet voice interrupts my rambling thoughts.

"I prefer fireman, snowflake." The way she says such a common term makes me feel like I really am a superhero.

She giggles and I return to my mission. In the apex of my thumb and forefinger, I squeeze while tugging down, mimicking Mr.

Renshaw's instructed motions. Then I almost fall off my rickety stool when the first spurt of milk hits my pail.

"Holy shit." As a man who prefers his milk cold and in aisle ten, this is surreal. Still, I keep up, eventually finding a steady rhythm. I am not as quick as the practiced Mr. Renshaw and his son, but I hold my own. By the time the gathered helpers are finishing up, I've milked eight cows on my own.

When the collective finishes, Mrs. Renshaw brings out donuts, hot and homemade, and big carafes of coffee and warm cider. Pear and I linger among the others, sipping our drinks, and sharing small talk. A sense of community I haven't experienced before weaves around us.

Sure, I have family, friends, and the firehouse, but this is different. I am not about to become a farmer, but the moment feels important, special. I'm honored to be part of this morning's accomplishment.

"Any time you need a favor, I'm your man," Mr. Renshaw says, clapping me on the back.

I didn't have any idea what I could possibly ask of him. Most likely, I wouldn't be back to this farm. However, my eye had caught on something just inside the barn when we first entered.

Clamping my hand on his shoulder, I lead him away from Pear.

"Actually, Mr. Renshaw, I was wondering if I could ask for that favor now."

And that's how Pear and I end up on a horse-drawn sleigh, riding through Mr. Renshaw's fields.

"This is incredible," Pear whispers like she'll disturb the two horses pulling us at a rhythmic trot.

Mr. Renshaw sits upfront while Pear and I huddle together in the back seat. A heavy quilt covers our laps. I have my arm around Pear, and she's tucked into my side. For the first few minutes of our ride, we didn't speak. We just enjoyed the quiet clopping of hooves crunching snow and the weak slushing of sled runners over the frozen ground. The fields slowly pass us or rather we slowly crawl over them. This is not a high-speed snowmobile. This vehicle is made for time. Not a rush, but patience.

If I thought Pear looked in her element milking a cow, she's practically vibrating with excitement as we sit in this sleigh.

"You're really digging this, aren't you?"

Pear shrugs beneath my arm. "I'm a modern woman but it doesn't mean I don't appreciate the simpler things in life. An older way of doing things."

"Do you know how long it would take you to get from here to Chicago in one of these things?"

Pear chuckles. "You *wouldn't* go from here to Chicago in a sleigh. This is for local travel. For visiting."

Suddenly, I picture Pear in a long wool coat with a muff at her hands, like some woman from a Charles Dickens classic. She's gone off for a secret rendezvous with some man her family disapproves of. They'd ice skate on a pond. Kiss behind evergreens. I'd be that bad boy in her life; however, there isn't a chance I can picture myself in the same scene.

I'm a modern man, through and through.

However, Pear is refreshing.

She makes pies for breakfast and chili feasts for game days.

She builds homes for owls and loves her dad unconditionally.

She has put up with me for eight days and I've never been so grateful.

Cupping her jaw in my gloved hand, I turn her head, so she faces me and kiss her. Long and sweet, slow but steady, like the movement of this antique sled.

Pear is a classic.

And again, I wish I could keep her, bringing her into the future with me.

day 9

nine ladies line dancing

January 3

chapter 16

[Pear]

I was starting to feel cooped up. Sure, we'd been on the snowmobile trail and visited Mr. Renshaw's farm, but I wanted to go out-*out*. I needed a break because my thoughts were getting too comfortable with Brock. The romantic gesture of a sleigh ride was my tipping point. For such a grouchy man, the request felt out of character. Then again, he'd brought me flowers, made me French toast, carved me a wooden snowflake and given me some amazing orgasms.

Were orgasms the only thing he'd give me? Could I have his heart?

On the ninth day, after Brock completed another list of menial tasks around Dad's place, I made a decision.

"We're going out," I announce as the heavy darkness of a winter evening fills the sky.

The closest town was a touristy place on the waterfront of Lake Michigan where we took the Polar Plunge. Just outside of town was a large barn-like country bar hosting a ladies' night.

The theme did not mean men could not attend. In fact, tons of men were present to scope out the large collection of women gathered with their friends for a night out. Some women I imagine were moms, looking to let lose a little after weeks of being cooped up with their school-aged kids. Other women might be single ladies on the prowl, hoping to turn ladies' night into one-night stands.

I'd taken myself out of that crowd a while ago. I wasn't a one-night kind of gal, which made whatever I was doing with Brock special.

He was special.

"Whatcha think, fireman?" My body vibrates with excitement. I love to dance, and I'd promised Brock a burger and a beer. We sit at a high-top table, our knees touching since he pulled my stool closer to his when we first took our seats.

"I'm not dancing."

I pout. He's such a spoilsport. However, the great thing about line-dancing is you don't need a partner. And when the ladies are called to the floor, I hop off my stool, eager to shake off this weird energy humming within me with some honky-tonk boogie.

A little to the left, to the left, and the right, and the right, then slide was doing wonders for my mood until I see a brunette standing close to our high-top table, laughing at something Brock said and placing her hand on his forearm.

I don't like it. Not one bit. I'd been a jealous lover with Reggie which was something I didn't like about myself. I should have felt confident in our relationship that he wouldn't cheat on me, and for the most part, money *had* been his mistress, not another woman. However, that didn't mean there weren't plenty of times when I felt inferior around Reggie. How women looked at him. How he watched them. How he eventually viewed me.

He'd told me I was fat. That alone should have told me his true feelings.

He didn't respect me or my body type.

He hadn't deserved my jealousy.

Still, a pinch of envy ripples through me as Brock leans toward the woman, speaking closer to her ear. I could write it off as the music being loud, but I refuse to make excuses for any man. For too long, I'd made them about Reggie and his issues.

Stepping away from the dancing ladies, I strut back to the table. Brock glances up at my approach. His smile curls the corner of his mouth before instantly falling at something he reads on my face.

"Snowflake?"

Don't fucking snowflake me. I'll burn this place down if he's flirting with another woman in front of me.

Brock chuckles roughly before introducing, "This is Anna. Anna McCaryn."

The woman's face blushes. "It's actually Anna Becker now." There's a story behind the brightness in her face but I don't ask, too busy seeing red thanks to his hand on her back as he introduces her.

"Anna and I went to high school together," Brock explains.

How convenient.

"And my family owns a house in Lakeside. Lakeside Cottage," she states as if I've heard of the place.

Sounds lovely.

"We've been kicked out for the week as my sister is in town from Chicago and using the place with a group of friends."

"Her younger sister, Amelia, went to school with my younger brother Zebb," Brock continues with this little reunion. His hand remains on her back.

"There you are." A devastatingly handsome man saunters up to the table. With brown wavy hair that curls around his ears and tickles the back of his neck, plus deep-set eyes, he's mouthwatering good-looking, but I'm still seeing violet because of Brock.

The man slips his arm around Anna's waist and tugs her into his side.

Anna and Brock repeat their shared history. I'm introduced to her husband, Mason. He doesn't seem any more excited to witness Brock touching Anna than I am.

Maybe it was all innocent. Maybe Brock is just a touchy-feely kind of man, but I don't care for it. His hands belong to me.

The thought is ridiculous. I can't be jealous. Envy is petty, confounding, and inconvenient. I don't even know if Brock would consider being all in with me. In just a few short days, we'll have only known each other for twelve days. That's not a lifelong relationship. That's a winter fling.

The thought sours my mood further.

"It was great to see you again," Anna eventually offers, lifting a hand and timidly waving at me. "Happy New Year."

"Happy New Year."

Mason reaches out a hand to shake Brock's before stepping over to me and kissing my cheek.

I watch as Mason's hand possessively lands on Anna's lower back, and he leads her away from our table. When I turn toward Brock, his eyes are laser focused on me.

"Care to explain what that was all about." He lifts his hand and waves a finger in a circle around my face.

I smack at his pointer, and he chuckles hard. "She's pretty. Former girlfriend?"

"Old friend. I took her to a dance in high school."

"Sounds fun." What I sound like is a bitter, jealous girlfriend who sees a beautiful woman aging well in her forties. Not that I'm aging poorly, it's just that she looks so good. Fit. Trim. *She's* lovely. And all fresh-faced and beaming with love for the man who proudly called himself her husband.

Brock runs his hand up my spine, but I stiffen beneath his touch. When his hand reaches the back of my neck, he holds still, squeezing at the spot. "What am I missing here?"

"You're a flirt, aren't you? I bet you go to bars and easily pick up women, don't you?"

His brows lift with shock before his eyes narrow. "Are you jealous?"

Standing taller, I shake out my shoulders and lift my head. "I have nothing to be jealous of," I counter with more confidence than I feel.

"Damn right you don't." Brock sighs, removing his hand from my neck, then slipping his fingers through mine and bringing my knuckles to his lips. "Look, we both have pasts. But that's where they should stay. Behind us. I'm not innocent but I have not been reckless, despite what the guys think of me. Despite what Cap has thought."

I watch as his eyes soften in the dim light of the country bar.

"I'm here with *you*, snowflake."

"But you were touching her," I remind him, sounding petulant and irritated.

Brock sighs, watching me. "You're right. I shouldn't have touched her." His tone turns serious. "I've been cheated on and I know how that can make you question yourself. Make you feel unwanted and insecure. Unloved and discarded. And I would never, ever want to make you feel that way, Paradise, even if inadvertently."

He softly chuckles. "I'd go apeshit if the roles were reversed."

His reassurance settles my simmering blood a little.

"Anna and I were old friends, and you and I are new."

One is silver and the other gold?

"Friends?" I scoff, my blood slowly heating again.

Brock tugs me closer to him and I stumble against his thigh until he spreads his legs and moves me between them. His hands fall to my hips, holding me in place while my gaze lowers to the buttons on his flannel shirt.

"Baby, look at me."

Slowly, I lift my head.

"What do you want us to be, Pear?"

I don't have a definition. I don't have a label. I just didn't want him to be with someone else. Not yet. We still have three more days before he will be set free. Before the truth will come out.

I have no right to play the jealous lover card.

"I . . . I don't know," I finally admit.

"Yeah, me neither." However, the corners of Brock's mouth slowly hitch up. "Still, is it wrong that I kind of like that you were jealous?" He inhales deeply, puffing out his chest. "Mama bird all ruffled over daddy. Like swans who are possessive of their mates. Feels good to be wanted like that."

While he jostles my hips, I weakly laugh, smacking at his firm pecs. "You're ridiculous." But I'm the one whose face heats, embarrassed by my behavior.

"Now, about me flirting . . . want me to flirt with you?"

"Lay it on me, fireman," I tease, relieved that we're back to being playful.

Brock eyes me a second, making a show of lowering his gaze, roaming up my body like he's tracing the outline of my solid thighs, my wider hips, and my firm breasts. I shiver beneath his assessment.

"You're a real fireball. Take a shot with me. Then take a shot on me."

"Weak," I chuckle, toying with the collar of his shirt.

"Give me a chance, snowflake. I bet I can make you melt. On my tongue." He sticks out his tongue.

"There is no way that line works on anyone."

"I don't need it to work on anyone. I only want you." His tone shifts to serious. The flirt is still present in his eyes, but the cheesy pickup lines are erased. He leans forward to kiss me, tantalizingly slow and sweet, simmering and making me melt after all. He's good at this.

"Gonna dance with me, cowboy?" I ask coyly, pulling back from him.

"Does milking cows once make me a cowboy?"

I laugh again while running my hand down his chest. "I doubt it. Besides, I prefer firemen."

Brock catches my hand dragging down his midsection and flattens it over his racing heart. "Fire*man*," he emphasizes. "Singular. Me."

My laughter deepens while my eyes remain focused on his. "Fine. You're the only one."

"Better," he grunts. "Now, let's dance."

Standing, he takes my hand again and leads me to the dance floor where Taylor Swift sings about lovers and Christmas lights in January.

I wish the holidays would never end.

day 10

ten logs for chopping

January 4

chapter 17

[Pear]

On day ten, Brock makes his own To-Do list, which includes splitting ten stumps he found that needed chopping to replenish our firewood stack.

He starts out in his winter jacket but quickly shifts to that heavy camel-colored sweater he wore earlier. Then he's down to only a flannel which hugs his form. Biceps bulging. Back muscles straining.

There is something ridiculously sexy about a man chopping wood.

The ax. The power. The split.

It so primeval and my body is on fire as I sip hot chocolate and watch him through the window.

This is better than reality television. It's reality.

And when the day ends, we're making our own heat again.

day 11

eleven pipin' pick-up (lines)

January 5

chapter 18

[Brock]

I'm grateful for the logs I split yesterday, because by midday, the power goes out. With weather warnings of six to forty-eight inches, which is quite a disparity in prediction, the outdoors has become a winter whiteout. We can't see more than a few centimeters out the windows, which rattle a little as the wind howls. The scene could be considered frightful, but inside is delightful, as the song goes.

"The day feels ripe for napping," Pear says, wandering up beside me near the window as the light inside the house fades. We haven't broken out candles, letting the blaze in the fireplace illuminate the room.

"I feel like I'm totally slacking," I counter. While Pear has given me list after list of items to complete, I've finished the tasks quicker each day, spending more time lingering in her company than working on projects.

I need a good report from Pear. Need to prove myself to Cap. I can't lose the fire department.

However, I am more concerned now that I'll lose Pear. She hadn't offered a definition for us the other night and I don't want to ask again. However, I really want to keep seeing her somehow.

"When do you return to Atlanta?" She'd told me she arrived on Christmas day, and the calendar has almost reached two weeks, a standard period of vacation leave.

"Oh. Uhm. About that?" She ducks her head and brushes hair around one ear. "I'm actually not returning."

"Really?" I clear my throat after the too-surprised and too-hopeful response. "I mean, really."

With her eyes fixated on the swirling snow outside the window, she explains, "I quit my job."

"What?" My shock cannot be contained. "Why?"

Pear sighs before offering a quick glance at me then returns her gaze to the window. "It's a long story."

"And we have time." When the power went out, a local outage notice came through our cell phones with no estimation on when the electricity will be restored. Glancing back toward the window, I estimate it won't be anytime soon, so we have plenty of time to discuss Pear's situation.

"I told you that Reggie had a gambling issue. He'd set us . . . me . . . back three years with his delinquent tax payments. I was grateful I had a job, and I was good at what I did, but I didn't love the place."

Pear has already told me she worked in sales for a major pre-packaged food distributor. They sold anything from frozen peas to fresh chicken.

"Anyway, around the time I'd made my final pay-off to the government my rental lease was coming to an end. We'd lost the house to collections. And I was ready for a change."

She waves down her body, emphasizing her outfit which is her loose-fit white pants and fuzzy white sweater along with thick cabin socks on her feet.

"Thus, the white," she reminds me. "But I knew I needed more than a wardrobe update. I needed a life shift. Plus, my boss is a dick."

I chuckle at her vehement dislike. "What'd he do?"

"He'd hit on me one too many times and I was tired of playing nice. I finally told him I was reporting him to HR if he didn't knock it off. Not to mention, his wife was sweet, and she didn't deserve someone like him in her life."

"You threatened him?"

"Not exactly." She continues to avoid looking at me.

"Well, tell me what *exactly*."

"Ever want to throat punch your boss?" Her voice lowers.

"Not literally." I choke, laughter in my tone again. My boss is her dad, and while I'd had my moments with Cap, and any other authoritative person, I'd never hit someone out of anger. What happened with Dane and me was a joke, outside of the department, and on our private time. However, the incident had created a ruckus within the department as a public display of aggression. Another strike against me.

"Well, I did." Pear finally turns to look at me.

"You mean you thought about throat punching him?" I ask to clarify but the churn in my stomach tells me there's more to the story.

"No. I throat punched him." She imitates by curling her middle finger and ring finger inward, making a bull-like formation with her forefinger and pinky. "Right to the Adam's apple."

"Jesus." I swallow hard as if I can feel the short, quick jab to my neck. "Why did you do that?"

"Because he grabbed my ass."

"What the fuck?"

"Yep. And that's when I told him I would report him to HR. After he threatened that he'd report me for assault, he told me I was fired. I told him he didn't have to fire me. I quit."

"Holy shit."

"Yeah." She sighs again. Her shoulders fall. Her arms cross over her chest. "Life implosion two-point-oh."

I wrap my arm around her shoulders and tug her against my side. "Does your dad know all this?" I'd like to assume Cap does, but somehow, I don't think so.

"Not yet." Her head falls forward again. "I was hoping to tell him everything when I got here." She slowly lifts her head, turning her face to me. "He doesn't know the half of it."

"What do you mean?"

"He knows Reggie and I divorced but he doesn't know about the money. I didn't want him to worry. I'd handled it. But now I'm free of that debt and that episode in my life, and I want a fresh start."

"Sounds like you're looking for a second chance, more than your life imploded a second time."

Pear weakly smiles. "Dad is going to be so angry about the details I held back, but I'm hopeful that by telling him I'm moving to Chicago, he won't be half as upset."

"You're moving to Chicago?" Clearly, this decision had been made before her arrival at the farm, before she met me, but a small part of me does a weird hop-skip-tap of my feet in mid-air because she isn't leaving. She'll be following me to Chicago.

Well, not following me but living there.

"Where will you live?"

"I was hoping to crash at Dad's for a little while. Not for long, though, as he only has two bedrooms, and the second room is an office slash den for him."

I've been to Cap's place. It's nice but small. The place will be cramped.

"Where is all your stuff?"

"In a storage pod, and in a holding pattern until I know where I'll live. My car, however, is being delivered to Chicago." She tips her arm and glances at her wrist like she's wearing a watch. "Today."

Pear peers out the window once more. Not a chance that delivery is being made if this winter storm is happening in Chicago.

"So, you came here to talk with Cap. Only he left for twelve days. But you'll be going home with him after he returns." My mind is bumbling through the steps, always arriving at the same result.

She is going to Chicago, too.

"That's the plan. For now."

"And what about a job? Do you have savings?"

Pear scoffs. "Not enough to live on. Reggie wiped me out. And I'd been holding out for a promised Christmas bonus that didn't happen. But even if I need to wait tables for a while, I'll do it. I just want time to rethink the direction my life has taken and then straighten the path toward something else."

"Like what? Do you have any ideas on what you'd like to do?" I'm boggled by all that I've heard.

She'd been harassed. She throat-punched her boss. She worked hard to dig out of a financial hole she hadn't dug in the first place and she's turning her life upside down to start over.

She was the superhero here. Not me.

"When I went into therapy for my head, I also started working out for my body. Not necessarily to lose weight but to help my heart, maybe slim some pounds, but also to build strength and stamina. In my limited free time, I've been working on becoming a certified fitness instructor. I want to help others understand our bodies are individual and unique, in whatever shape or size that might be. What isn't normal is everything else we learn about how we *should* look or what we *should* wear. Even what we should or shouldn't eat. It's about finding happiness within one's self, and honestly, fuck everyone else."

Happiness. She'd mentioned the emotion before when we discussed Nick and what he might do with *his* life. Not that a job was the end all, be all of happiness. Joy was the important part, especially when you spent eight to twelve hours of your day working.

If one-third of your time applies to employment, shouldn't that job be worth your time?

Scoffing at her desire to be a fitness instructor would be insensitive. She'd been making six-figures, and she wanted to downsize to an hourly-wage, but I'd learned the hard way that money does not equate happiness.

Time should. The time you spend at work. The time you give to others. The time you are alone.

Time is more valuable than money.

You can spend time, but you can never recoup it. You can't save it up. You can't earn more.

You only have the time that is given to you, which is *your* life, and it should not be wasted.

With that thought, I cup the back of Pear's neck. "I think being a certified fitness instructor in Chicago sounds like a great idea." I might even know a guy or two who could help her out. Find her a gym. Recommend individuals to be trained. It was all do-able, and it meant a future for her. And maybe for us.

I kiss her slowly at first, but the crackling energy around us quickly builds like the roaring fire in the stone hearth. With the power out, only the dancing glow of the flames skittering among the logs illuminates the room.

Pear shivers.

"Are you cold?" I rub my hands up and down her arms. The heat in the house has been slowly diminishing while the temp in this front room remains relatively consistent.

"I'm okay," Pear lies as another shiver ripples through her.

"I have an idea." Leaving her for a moment, I go to her bedroom and remove all the quilts and blankets from the bed, tucking the pillows underneath my arms as well. Returning to the living room, I spread out a blanket and then position the dining room chairs in a formation that supports another blanket over the top of the high backs, forming a blanket igloo.

I toss the pillows inside the space and return to Cap's room for more pillows and blankets.

With our cozy den complete, Pear and I crawl inside, and the heat centralizes around us.

"I haven't made a blanket fort in forever." Pear stares overhead at the blanket design above us. "If only we had fairy lights."

The miniature lights would add to the ambiance, but I like the atmosphere. We agreed to conserve our phone batteries by shutting off the devices, only turning them on once each hour to check weather reports. In the meantime, we have quite the romantic setting with the fire blazing and the blanket tent surrounding us.

I want this cocoon around us to stop time and make Pear mine.

"Since you're planning to be a certified fitness instructor, I was wondering if you could help me with my flexibility," I flirt, running the tip of my finger up her arm.

"Is this another one of your weak pickup lines?" she flirts back.

"Do I need a pickup line?"

Pear shifts to her side, facing me. "You could still *try* to woo me."

"Woo you?" I huff, good-natured.

"Lay it on thick. Let's see what you got."

"Okay." I smirk. "Countdown on."

"Countdown? Like when the clocks kept rolling into a new year?"

And I kissed her until we were both balls of sexual energy, ready to burst. I shake my head. "This is a countdown to all the things I cherish about you."

Pear blinks in surprise. *Game on.*

"Have I told you how heavenly you are, Paradise?"

She rolls her eyes.

"How you're like a ripe pear that needs to be savored."

"Weak," she mutters but a smile curls her mouth.

I shift, sitting upright to remove one of her thick socks and then the other. "How you might have once dressed like a dark turtle but you're more like a white dove, offering peace, penance, and compassion."

"Brock." She laughs until her eyes catch on mine.

I crawl over her and reach for the hem of her shirt, removing her arms before tugging the sweater over her head. "You're solid like a fence post."

"A fence—"

I cut off her disgruntled sound with a finger over her lips. "Strong. Resilient. A survivor. You've stood up to a lot over the years, but tonight, I want you to relax. Let me be in charge."

"Okay." She swallows hard and licks her lips.

"Do you know what I thought when we stood beneath the stars and listened to the owls?"

Pear shakes her head on the pillow while I pull down her pants and tug a blanket over her cool skin.

"*Who*"—I coo—"is this woman and how can I win her over?" *Win her heart.*

I fold to my side beside her and prop up on my arm. Using my finger, I trace down her nose and around her eyes, before trailing over her lips.

"We have five senses and yet they aren't enough. Not only do I want to taste and touch, see and smell and hear you, but I want to feel you. I want to be inside you." I drag my finger over her heart and tap twice.

"Fireman," she whispers the nickname with awe, but she has no idea the adoration I have for her. What she's dealt with. What she's overcome. I promised her I'd get some mental help, and I'll hold to that vow. I want to work on me. I want to be better for her.

"Did you know there are six pleasure points on the body?" I lean forward for her mouth. "Here." The kiss is only a sip as I have more areas to count on her body.

"And here." I run my finger along the column of her throat, and she tips her head, allowing me to press another kiss there.

Tugging down the blanket I'd wrapped over her chest, I pluck at a taut nipple peaking underneath her bra. "Here too." I move to the other breast to give that nipple a tweak as well.

Pear does not disappoint as she arches her back, as if desiring that I linger longer but I have more places to travel along her body.

Pushing more of the blanket off her, I run my hand up her inner thigh and she easily spreads her legs.

"These." I hum as she knows how much I love her solid legs.

"Of course, here," I add, reaching around her and cupping her ass as I wedge myself between her calves.

"And the final spot." I blow a hot breath over her covered pussy.

Pear whimpers. "I think that was seven."

"Math isn't my strong suit." I run my nose along her panties, inhaling the musky scent of her arousal. "But if seven is a lucky number, you're my number one."

A moment passes before Pear figures out that math equation. "You're my number one, too."

I smile before pressing a kiss to her warm heat, but I'm not done counting all the ways I adore her.

"Eight," I blurt.

"Eight what?"

"The number of years I've been waiting for someone like you." There'd been five years since my divorce but three years of misery before it was final. And I've been holding off from committing to anyone new because *my girl* was out there, somewhere, waiting on me.

Now, we're here.

"Brock," Pear whispers, her voice thick. Her delicate hand cups my cheek so I'm forced to hold on her eyes which glisten. So beautiful. So breathtaking. So full of hope, and I never want to disappoint her.

"Are you a cat?" I tease, popping the intensity of our stare. "I have nine lives I'd like to live with you."

Pear laughs, deep and rich and curling at the waist as I jest with words I intend seriously. I think I've been waiting for *her* my entire life. For so long, I've been too afraid to admit it, to recognize this yearning inside me. Too frightened I've missed my chance at happiness. Too scared to hope happiness was still out there for me.

"Ten." I pop up to all fours and grab her hand, sucking each finger on her left before moving to her right. As I lower toward her feet, she squeals.

"You wouldn't dare."

"Suck your toes?" I sure fucking would and when I clamp my teeth around her pinky one, she stills. I give each toe a nip before running my hands up her legs. Her firm ankles. Her solid calves. Her thick thighs.

"Perfect," I hum, reaching her hips and tugging at her underwear, dragging it down her body to remove it. "You're an eleven on a scale of one to ten."

"That might be the cheesiest line yet."

However, the next sound out of her is a gasp as I lick her seam, splitting her open to shove my tongue between her lower lips, and kiss her. Her fingers slide through my hair, gently yanking at the short ones on the back of my head. The sharpness spurs me on.

I sip and I suck. I dip and I devour. She's a Christmas surprise and a New Year's celebration. And I want her for every holiday in between the start of a new year and the end.

For now, I take my time to bring her to the crest and tip over the edge. When her legs stiffen and then her thighs clap on the sides of my head, I double down my worship of her body until she's champagne overflowing a cup and bubbling on my tongue. Until she cries out my name and moans with an unsung hallelujah.

Once spent, I climb back up her body and sit back to hastily remove my flannel shirt and the thermal I wear underneath, then I roll to the side to kick off my jeans and boxer briefs. In no time, I'm between her thighs again.

"Is this okay?" I ask, fisting myself, long and stiff, and desperate to be inside her.

"Condom? I'm on the pill, but still . . . condom."

I scramble backward, pulling out the few packets I shoved in my jeans pocket. I hadn't planned on this happening during my twelve-day retreat. The condoms were in my duffle bag, and I've never been so grateful as when I'd found them there the other day.

As I roll on the condom, I watch Pear slide her fingers between her legs.

"You startin' without me, snowflake?"

"Keeping myself warm for you."

Fuck. She's going to be the death of me. A heavenly one.

With her thighs spread and cradling me between them, I line myself up once more.

"You set the pace, baby. I can go fast or slow. I can be rough or sweet. Your call."

"Yes." One single word gives me permission to do it all.

But first, I slide forward, watching as her body welcomes me inside her indescribable heat. Her opening is soaked, and I easily glide inward, awed as I disappear within her.

"Snowflake," I choke at the stranglehold she has on me. Clenching me tight within her. "Fuck, you feel so good."

"The best," she groans, tipping back her head and arching her back as if she can draw me deeper.

I'm almost to the hilt and I pull back, teasing to withdraw completely when her hands clap on my shoulder blades. Her fingertips scratch down my back, inching toward my ass.

I surge forward and we both gasp.

"Fuck," I moan.

"Yeah," she whimpers.

In and out I move, bringing myself to the brink and then rushing home to fill her. Pear's body chases mine, letting me retreat before squeezing to keep me inside, trapping my head with a hold so tight I never want her to let go. I thrust inward, setting a rhythm of long pulls and quick pushes until we're both a mess of sweaty skin and ragged breaths.

"I want to feel you break around me."

"Brock," she cries out, kneading her fingers into my backside, spreading my cheeks apart. With her legs spread wide and her knees raised, I grab her shin and tug her leg toward her chest, opening her up to me.

"Yes," she groans.

My body detects what I've learned about hers before this moment. How her legs stiffen. As if all the pressure collides in one spot before she combusts, falling into the release like the burst of a firework, lighting up the sky before floating back down to the ground. Sated and spent.

Her head falls back, and I wait out the final flicker of her flame before building up my own inferno, rocking into her harder, diving deeper.

"Pear," I strain. After the way she was milking my dick, I'm going to spill any second. With a final clench from her, my dick gives out and I release on a sudden jolt. Pinpricks of light dance before my eyes, blinding me for a second. I can't do anything but feel her around me. The slickness of her release. The tension of her channel, and the warmth of her cradling me inside her, embracing my own explosion.

My forehead falls to the pillow just above her shoulder as my breath comes ragged and quick. My heart hammers in my chest while my thoughts race.

Only one thing is clear. I've fallen for this woman.

Similar to the blizzard outside, I've lived my life like a raging storm, only to be calmed by the stillness of one snowflake.

Pear turns her head on the pillow and kisses just below my ear. Her lips against my sensitive skin are delicate, sweet, and innocent.

And the bastard that I am, I want to steal all her goodness and keep it for myself.

175

chapter 19

[Pear]

We doze.

What else is there to do after such satisfying sex on a blizzardy afternoon? The wind whirls. The windows occasionally rattle. But in our blanket igloo, Brock and I nuzzle together, and nap.

Admittedly, if I had been here alone, I would have been frightened. The house is old and creaks, and while the fireplace was keeping us cozy, I don't think I ever would have had enough chopped wood without Brock's presence.

As I slowly stir, I watch him sleep. His sturdy nose flares as he breathes softly. With his eyelids closed, the length of his lashes is more apparent against his cheeks. The silver in his beard is solid white in patches. He's strikingly handsome and I hesitantly hover my fingertip over his lips, mentally tracing them to store in my memory.

Tomorrow is day twelve and he'll be anxious to go home. He's told me how his kids are waiting, as much as college age-kids want to hang with their parents. Nick sounds like a firecracker like his father but kind and loving toward his sister. No less than it sounds like Brock is toward his own sister, Marnie, and her wife, Lisa. When Brock mentions Ellie, his face lights up, nearly blushing with love for his daughter. According to him she's perfect, but I remember being eighteen. She has her flaws somewhere her father will never see them.

I'm reminded of myself. All the things I tried to protect my father from knowing. When I was younger, my sister was there to lean on when I made mistakes.

The boy I gave my virginity to in my senior year of high school.

The kid in my psychology class who broke my heart, ghosting me after two months.

The guy I'd hoped to marry before I met Reggie.

Precious never met Reggie. If she had, she might have instantly discerned he wasn't good enough for me. No one ever had been.

But Brock . . . she would have adored him. The quiet things he did, like pulling out my chair or holding open a door. The handmade wooden snowflake he'd taken the time to carve himself. The way he stuck out his restorative sentence, embracing these twelve days in order to prove himself to my dad.

"I can feel you watching me," he mumbles, groggy and grouchy, but without any bite. Slowly, his mouth curls before his lids open. "Hi."

"Hi." I swallow around a sudden lump in my throat. One chalky and jagged like a lump of coal. "I need to tell you something."

It was time to fess up. He needed to know that Dad—

"Me too," he grumbles before scooting closer to me and kissing me without further warning. His fingers tighten on my hip, tugging me to him despite blankets falling between us.

"Brock," I mutter against his lips, internally chastising myself after taking eager sips of him. "I—"

"I had a dream about you."

He cuts me off once more, returning his mouth to mine, kissing me senseless before I finally ask, "What was the dream?"

"Let me show you."

Brock shoves back the blankets wrapped over our bodies. The sudden rush sends a shiver over my skin as the cool air hits us. The fire has lost its blaze, settling into embers that sizzle and hiss. We'll need to stoke it again, but Brock has other plans.

He reaches for my wrists and tugs me upright. "Let's play a game."

I chuckle softly as I'd suggested the same thing during the college football game, wagering sexual favors for winning quarters. I wasn't a gambler, but I loved a good competition and a competitive gleam fills Brock's eyes. He retrieves a deck of cards that I hadn't noticed from beneath the pillows.

"Pick a card." He holds out two.

I'm curious while hesitant to play along, wavering between the two cards, one pushed forward a few millimeters compared to the other. Whether on purpose or not, I exaggerate my decision making.

"Do I want this one?" I pause before what looks like the shorter of the two. "Or this one?" Hovering my eager fingers in front of the longer one.

I glance up at Brock but he's no help, his face stoic and firm. When I pull forward the shorter one, certain he wants me to take the longer of the two, I watch his face once more. He'd be great at poker. Considering we are already naked, though, this definitely isn't a game that involves stripping off our clothes.

"Perfect," Brock states, taking my wrist and turning my hand so my card faces him.

The queen of diamonds.

"Did you know that the fifty-two cards in a deck represent the weeks of the year?"

No. At forty-one years old, I had no idea and I stare at him, uncertain where this is going.

"Four suits for four seasons. Winter, spring, summer, fall. Thirteen cards each representing the number of weeks within them."

"Phew." I whistle. "Maybe you are more country than city after all," I tease, as the seasons are agricultural in nature.

"And you've drawn the queen of diamonds, which represents summer. She's feminine." Brock circles my wrist and rubs his thumb up my inner forearm. "The diamond is actually a vulva."

My head pops up. "You're making this up."

He shrugs. "I'm not." The corner of his mouth ticks upward and I don't know if he's serious or teasing, but stroking my inner arm suggests where this game is leading.

"She's strength and wealth, and lots of orgasms in your future."

I laugh, lifting my chin. "And what's your card?"

With a flick of his fingers, he presents his card to me. "King of Clubs."

"Which means?"

"Winter. The club symbolizes the three-in-one spirit. But also represents strength and determination."

"And lots of orgasms in *your* future," I tease.

Brock's expression remains serious while his eyes are playful.

"What kind of game are we playing here? And how does this relate to your dream?"

Brock reaches around me, patting the seat of the dining chair that faces inward. "You sit on this throne, and I worship you."

I glance from the seat to Brock's face, wondering once more what he's playing at but as he gently nudges me to the chair, I follow his lead, giving into his game.

All desire to talk has left my brain. Especially when Brock spreads my knees, forcing my center to be exposed to him in a way I've never been, and I pulse in all the places.

Brock pins my legs open, my thighs over the front corners of the high-back chair. The woven cane seat beneath my bare bottom takes a second to adjust to. The blanket overhead brushes against my hair, but the second Brock's hot breath hits that tender spot, naked and visible to him on his knees before me, all thoughts are forgotten.

He worships me as he promised, like the alpha king he is, making me feel like his queen. His tongue is sin. His lips redemption. And those teeth . . . good God, I don't know how he does it, but his teeth have skill as he teases my flesh. Then it's tongue and lips again, and my legs shake.

At first, I'm combing my fingers through his hair, but eventually I need to steady myself as my knees bounce. I reach behind me, gripping the sides of the seat for stability as my backside balances on the edge.

Brock hums as he feasts. His eager moans and happy groans fill our little tent. Our bubble of paradise. The blanket den of amorous congress.

"Fireman," I groan, gritting my teeth as I near the brink.

"Don't come," Brock pulls back, growling his demand before dipping his tongue into me once more.

"What?" I choke. I can't hold back. I'm too close. My toes are tipped on the floor. My legs violently quake. I'm a bundle of nerves and then—

Brock moves away.

"No," I moan, tipping back my head before peering at Brock, glaring daggers at him.

However, Brock has risen on his knees, bringing his magnificent length to meet that sensitive nub, the tip manually guided to slide up and down in the slippery mess his mouth has made of me.

"I want you to let me in."

"Brock," I whimper.

"With nothing between us."

This would only be our second time. *What's the rush?* Still, I meet his eyes, reading more in them. He doesn't just mean physically. He wants me to let him into my heart. My secrets and my soul.

When I take too long to answer, Brock pulls back, lowering to his haunches, reaching his free hand for his pants somewhere in the pile of clothes and blankets.

I catch his forearm to stop him. "I trust you."

His eyes shift. No longer black as coal. No longer liquid ink. Something softer, like dark silk.

Rising back up on his knees, he cups my jaw with one hand. "I promise I'm not dangerous." He made that declaration once before to me. When I opened the door to him and decided to let him into the house. When I allowed him to stay for my own reasons.

I'd replied then that I doubted him. Because something deep inside warned me right then that if I let Brock Scroggs stay, he'd be dangerous for my heart.

However, my body is in control at the moment, and when the tip of his cock slips through slick folds, I watch as he disappears into me. As my body draws him into my depths and we become one.

Brock watches as well, hissing at the warmth of me surrounding him. Once he's to the hilt, he reaches around me, covering my hands clutching at the chair's edge. He pulls back and rocks forth, observing where our bodies join. His expression is full of wonder.

Completely vulnerable to Brock in this position, I'm unable to surge forward to meet his thrusts for fear the chair will topple. He keeps a steady pace, slowly rebuilding the lost orgasm, but I'm still afraid I won't tip over in this position.

"I don't think . . ." I'm hesitant to meet his eyes.

Without questioning me, Brock places a hand on my lower belly and stretches his thumb for the place I need him. With the thick pad of his thumb, he rubs in delicious circles on that tender spot, and I tremble once more. My feet catch on the rung of the chair, lifting my knees and opening me wider. I can't be any more exposed than I am. It's both freeing and frightening what this man is doing to me.

I'm a sexual goddess. The queen of diamonds. And Brock worships me in a ritual as old as true loves giving gifts for twelve days after Christmas.

"Brock," I whisper, uncertain what to say to him. Knowing I haven't told him a truth he needs to hear.

Selfish.

But when he flicks that delicate nub and thrusts forward in a way that causes my breath to hitch, I'm only in the moment. No past. No future. Just these moments in time, making a memory.

"I want you to come around me," Brock whispers, reverent, awed. Like he can't believe this is happening.

I'm not certain I can believe it either.

Still, I reach the tipping point, like the precarious edge of a diamond, and tumble over. I release the chair and clutch at Brock, holding onto him as my body fully takes over and I melt into the seat. The rush through my body is like the blizzard outdoors, only full of heat and jittery feelings swirling around me.

Lust. Love. Completion.

How can this man be three things at once?

The king of clubs.

This is quite the card game, and one of us needs to fold before we collapse. Before hearts are bruised.

"Paradise," Brock hisses, finding his own release, surging inward and jetting off inside me. He clamps his hands on my backside and tightens his hold, pinning me to him. His face buries in my neck. His breath is ragged and deep, and then he's peppering me with kisses. A trail along the column of my throat and down to my shoulder, then across my collarbone and finally up to my lips.

When he pulls back those dark eyes sparkle and gleam, like the diamond hidden beneath coal, ready to burst forth and show its worth.

He kisses me once more, before slowly releasing from me.

A quick reach for his shirt catches any mess before I excuse myself for the bathroom. The tiled space is freezing with the heat's absence, but the cool air feels momentarily refreshing.

Our blanket igloo grew a little intense. The intimacy almost too much for me. Words I shouldn't be saying eleven days after meeting a man tickle the back of my throat.

I'm in love with Brock.

I know it. Recognize it. Acknowledge it. Because this is a feeling I've never felt before, and that's why Brock Scroggs is dangerous.

+ + +

When I return to our huddle, restored from the blanket collapsing over our heads sometime during our sexual adventure on the chair, Brock has a plate of cheeses and meats, plus crackers and fruit beside him.

"I'm starving and I guess we should empty the fridge of what we can."

I fold down beside him, wearing a flannel shirt that he'd left in my room since he's been sleeping in there with me.

"Sounds like a plan." I try to keep my voice steady, although I don't know why it's shaking.

Brock doesn't catch the tremor. "You said you had something to tell me." His voice lowers while he reaches for a piece of cheese, setting a slice of sausage on top of it and placing both on a cracker.

"It can wait." I have one more day, I guess.

Twenty-four more hours to play my devious hand.

day 12

twelve thunderclouds

thunderin'

January 6

chapter 20

[Pear]

"Pear?"

Sitting bolt upright, I turn to Brock, conked out beside me. Through the slim opening of the blanket fort above us, the fire has dwindled to a dull orange of simmering embers once again.

Last night we went another few rounds of coming together between drifts of sleep and an actual card game. Each time one of us brushed up against the other, it was as if a match struck, and the flame sparked. We'd been insatiable.

Now, the bright light of a new day fills the chilly room.

And my dad is back early. Or is it late? *What time is it?*

"Dad." I hold my breath, hoping I'm dreaming. This cannot be happening. At forty-one years old, I'm *not* being caught in a blanket fort in the living room, minus my clothes, and lying beside someone who works with my father.

"Paradise?" My father's tone stiffens.

Nope. Not dreaming. Mortified, but not dead.

"Shit," I mutter, searching for clothing but when I can't seem to piece together anything that would semblance an outfit, I drag a quilt around me, exposing more of Brock before crawling out of the fort on all fours. Awkwardly I stand, with the blanket wrapped around my middle and clutching at it near my breasts.

"You're back early."

"With the storm finally over, I left hoping to beat another one." Dad is dressed in his typical winter attire. A quilted flannel and a knit cap covering his gray buzz cut. Weathered skin shows his age but his smile is typically warm. A thin layer of scruff covers his jaw from days without a razor. He turns his face toward the window before looking back at me. "I'm surprised you're still here."

"Where else would I be?" I told him I was sticking around for a while, playing off the extended time like this was a vacation, before I could tell him this was a permanent leave of absence from my former life.

Suddenly, the fort beside me shudders and the blanket over the top of the chairs collapses to cover Brock in a makeshift kilt around his waist. He stands to his full height and places his palm on my lower back, like a united front. He addresses my dad.

"Morning, Cap."

"Brock?" My father's gaze pings between the two of us before his brows crease, the divot severe enough to hold a quarter. "What are you doing here?"

Not exactly the first question I thought he'd ask, considering we're both only dressed in blankets.

"What do you mean?" Brock stares at my dad before giving me a questioning glance then looking back at Dad. "You told me to stay."

Dad's eyes narrow, his glare returning to me. "You got my text, right?"

I swallow hard and lower my head. Chewing at my lower lip, I side-eye Brock. This isn't how I wanted him to find out.

"What text?" Brock asks, rubbing up my back and watching me, before peering at my dad for answers.

"I'd messaged Pear later that first day, telling her she didn't have to keep you here. She'd been right. It wasn't fair to ask her to take on my responsibility. It was my job to restore you. It was your job to be on time and you hadn't been."

Brock removes his hand from my back, and I hate the loss of his touch. He swipes the same hand through his messy hair. His shoulders stiffen as my father continues to glare at him.

"I don't understand." Brock's voice is rough, from both sleep and sudden irritation. He scratches beneath his chin next, the hair thick along his throat. I don't want to think about where his face has been.

"I don't either," Dad counters, keeping his focus on Brock while taking a good look at him from top to toe. In our blanket attire, the situation is rather obvious.

"Dad, I can explain."

"You better explain." Dad points at Brock, ignoring me and focusing an accusing scowl in Brock's direction. He takes a step closer to us where Brock stands beside me, but I don't miss the incremental shift. The moment he slides a little bit away from me.

I rush forward. "Dad, it wasn't his fault."

"Whose was it then?" Brock asks from behind me.

I hang my head before looking back at him. "Mine."

"Explain this to me." Brock's hands come to his hips, his eyes are liquid ink again, on the verge of returning to dark coal. Questions well in his gaze, when I haven't worked out the answers yet.

I didn't really know why I did what I've done.

"You seemed so desperate for a chance to prove yourself to Dad." My voice falters.

"Are you turning this around on me?" Brock snaps, poking one thick finger against his bare chest. "I could have gone home, is that right?"

Brock looks up at Dad. Neither Dad nor I answer, as Dad's gaze shifts to me, brows cinched deeply in confusion. And disappointment.

I scramble to explain myself, keeping my gaze on Brock who refuses to look at me.

"When my dad sent a text that I could send you home, I intended to send you packing. But when you came to the door, all huffing and puffing about not finding a motel, I . . ." *I what?* Let him in. Made a space for the big bad wolf.

"You took advantage of me," Brock whispers, his gaze floating to me and holding.

"Not what it looks like from my perspective," Dad interjects, disgruntled and verging on his own example of an angered wolf.

"But I didn't," I say to Brock, my voice rising as I step in his direction again. "Look at all you did in twelve days. You gave owls a home and helped some cows. You donated to the Special Olympics and aided a farmer. You fixed Dad's fence and a few pieces of furniture."

My gaze shifts to Dad whose brows lower only a little. His expression shifting from upset father to puzzled mentor.

"Don't forget making Valentine's pears and chopping wood," Brock mocks.

"Valentine's pears?" Dad questions and I turn toward him.

"Brock put in his twelve days, Dad. He should be exonerated or considered restored or whatever you call it. He agreed to attend future therapy sessions."

"That's none of his business," Brock snaps again, fire and smoke in his words.

"You did?" Dad asks, glancing over my shoulder at his charge.

When I shift once more, Brock ignores Dad. The full weight of his cold stare is on me.

"Explain *this* to me." Brock points at the fallen fort. The heap of blankets that was once our little haven.

This is where it gets complicated. This is where I didn't want to hurt him, but I was tired of hurting. *Selfish*.

"It's the loneliest time of the year," I whisper. Sometimes a girl just wants her daddy. My one safe place but he was leaving for twelve long days.

Brock's brows hitch then crease.

I lower my voice when I say, "And I thought you seemed lonely, too."

That divot between Brock's brows turns into a deep furrow. "So you thought you'd . . . what? Lead me on? Take advantage of me? Let me hang out thinking I was working on myself only to learn you were working me instead."

"Hey," Dad snaps, causing me to flinch.

"It wasn't like that." But my voice is too weak, the defense even weaker. His explanation might sum it up. I didn't want to be alone, but I shouldn't have told him he could stay.

Hanging my head once more, I say quietly, "I didn't intend to trick you."

"Trick me?" Brock barks. "You made me fall—" A dark glare accompanies his abrupt stop. The silence that follows his unfinished sentence weighs as heavy as snow clouds around all of us.

"No one *makes* us do anything," With his hands on his hips, holding his disappointment momentarily at bay, Dad's advice is ill-timed. He means well but he needs to read the stormy room.

Brock turns on him. "Yeah, that's not what happened here. I thought I *had* to stay."

"You were late," Dad reminds him, his tone sharpening at the edge in Brock's voice. "You were free to go. In fact, you're now free from the department."

I step closer to my father again, hand up in defense. "Dad. *No.*"

Without a glance back at Brock, I feel the energy leave his body. His retorts. His defense. His fight. All gone. His anger is the only thing palpable in the room, swirling around me like yesterday's blizzard. A different kind of snowstorm, complete with frigid air and relentless emotions, seeps into my bones along with a bitter frost that numbs my flesh.

"Dad. Please." I beg, finally reaching him and forcing him to focus his   upset   on   me. "This is on me. I did this. I kept him here."

Dad stares at me, long and hard, and hurt. Behind me, I sense Brock shift, the damage to him done. He exits the room.

I squeeze my dad's shoulder before releasing him, clutching at my blanket dress again. "Dad," I whisper, uncertain how to plead Brock's case.

Dad's gaze momentarily drops to my attire before looking away, purposely keeping his eyes off me. "Are you trying to tell me you seduced that man?" His tone rings incredulous.

Now, I'm pissed. At Dad. At the situation. At myself for the sudden doubts his question raises.

"Why would that be so hard to believe?" Because I'm not thin and tiny. Because I've been divorced and devastated. Or rather, deceived. Because I'm a woman, I can't be a seductress.

"I just . . ." Dad swallows thickly. "You're not like that."

"Like what, Dad? Sexy? Smart? Knowing what I want and going after it." I sigh, and step back, giving myself distance from the one man I thought would love me in any form. "I didn't have the intention to fall for Brock. I didn't set out to *seduce him.*"

I hiss the words like the concept is something inconceivable, when it's actually been empowering. Maybe I unknowingly seduced him. Maybe I wanted him to be attracted to me, and he was. Maybe I'm a grown-ass woman and can own my sexuality however I see fit.

Not that I want to discuss my sexual escapades with my father, but I want him to understand I'm a woman. A woman with a brain and a body. A heart and desires. I deserve what I want. Maybe not by deceptive measures, of course, but I can still crave things *and* earn them.

"Fall for him?" Dad chokes.

"And why would *that* be so hard to believe?" I glare at my father, seeking his eyes. "You said yourself Brock is a good man with a big heart. You've given him chance after chance because you see something in him. Maybe you don't like his temper or his reactive behavior, but you also know he's been through a lot."

Dad mirrors my glare, surprised that I know a thing or two about Brock.

His divorce. His empty nest. His guilt over the loss of a fellow fireman.

Dad didn't get divorced, but he lost his wife. He lost his girls. One to death; one to a move. He's lost people beneath his command. Surely, he understands.

"And what about you, Pear? You've been through enough, too." He means Mom and Precious. Even Reggie.

"And I'm working on myself." I sigh. "And isn't that what you always taught me. Own up to mistakes. That's what your restorative sessions are about." And I've owned up to mine. Reggie being the biggest one, but not Brock.

"I feel like I don't know who you are right now."

"I have so much to tell you," I admit. But maybe after a shower. At the very least, I need to get dressed before I confess everything to my dad. Most of all, I want to talk to Brock. Still, I say, "But know this for now. I'm me, Dad. More me than I've felt in a long, long time." I swallow around a growing thickness in my throat. "I'm whole again."

Meeting my dad's concerned eyes, I add, "And Brock just wants to get there as well." I exhale. "Please don't take the department from him."

Dad's shoulders fall and he lowers his head a second before it pops up and he stares over my shoulder.

The hairs on the back of my neck prickle. *How long has Brock been standing there?*

Slowly, I turn to face him. He's fully dressed, his bag in his hand, ready to leave. His head is lowered as well, and I feel safe to assume he's heard quite a bit of my confession to my father.

Silently, he steps closer to me and pauses. My heart hammers. My breathing erratic. Brock inhales, closes his eyes a second and then opens them. Flames fire off around those coal-colored eyes.

"I'm so mad at you," he admits.

"I know," I whisper, my voice shaky. Tears prickle my eyes and Brock blurs before me, but I blink several times. The tears are for me. *My* loss of him. "I'm so, so sorry."

Brock nods once, leans toward me and weakly kisses my cheek. I close my eyes and a tear slips free. He doesn't address my dad, just passes his captain—former captain—and stalks to the pegs near the front door, removing his jacket and slipping into his construction boots.

Without a glance back at either of us, I watch through the kitchen window as Brock walks to his truck. Deciding I can't watch him drive away, I turn my head.

And by some freak of nature, the electricity clicks back on.

Too bad the sudden light does not touch the places that are dark and cold inside me.

chapter 21

[Brock]

Sometimes the quiet click of a closed door says more than a slammed one, and as I exit my captain's farmhouse and leave my heart shattered among the blankets on the living room floor, I climb into my truck, tossing my bag across the seat.

"Dammit," I holler into the cold cab, noticing my hands are shaking as I fumble in my pocket for the key fob. Once the ignition starts, I grip the steering wheel with both hands, letting the cold seep into my bare palms.

Glancing in the rearview mirror, I see a school bus painted in a pear-green color with Paradise Farms on the side.

How did he get that up the drive? Yesterday's blizzard raged through the night. A school bus couldn't have gotten up the gravel lane to the house. Still, I see a path plowed up the lane to the front of the barn where the bus is parked. I never heard a plow.

It's then that I realize I walked through a deep pile of snow to get to my truck and icy clumps are slithering into my boots. And still, I don't shake off the chill racing through my insides.

She tricked me. She used me. All those projects. All these days.

I was still having trouble processing everything.

Her dad waking us up. Her admitting she had feelings for me. Her defending herself . . . and me to Cap.

I scrub a hand over my face. *Fuck*. The scent of her is still on my skin. The taste of her on my tongue.

I have half a mind to rush back into the house. But I'm angry. She deceived me, strangely reminding me of my ex, although we weren't talking about dollars and cents here. We were talking about hearts.

Pear's and mine.

Hell, just yesterday I woke from a dream to find her staring at me. When she said she had something to tell me I thought she was about to express her regrets. Tell me she never wanted to see me again. Or couldn't see me after the twelve days were served. Tell me she had fun while I fucked her but we were over.

The toll of a bell rang in my head, signaling the end, and I panicked. I didn't let her speak. Instead, I wanted every last minute, every last drop, every last kiss to be spent with me.

Hadn't I been deceitful as well? As I made her pick a card and set her on that wobbly chair, making her think we were playing a game when I'd been honest in all I said. Laying all my cards out for her to read. Handing her my emotions.

I wanted to worship her. I'd do anything she asked, but I couldn't let her lie to me, and this is where I struggled.

Had she lied? She never said her dad gave her a list, only that *she'd* made a list. Fixing dresser drawers and mending fences. Building owl houses and making memories on a snowmobile. Plunging into frigid water and plucking at cow teats, all for her.

But it'd been good for me as well.

She even panicked at one point. She thought I'd left her when I went to the grocery store, reminding me when I returned that I could leave at any time. She wasn't holding me captive.

Still, I stayed. And as much as I want to say I did it for me, to prove something to Cap, I didn't want to go. I didn't want to leave her.

I was lonely. You seemed lonely, too.

"Fuck," I yell to the empty truck cab as the fog of my own breath fills the windows. A steaming bull trapped inside this vehicle.

She hadn't been wrong. I was lonely. Or I had been until twelve days ago.

If she'd told me upfront, maybe I wouldn't have stayed. I had my own issues to resolve, but then she became my resolution.

My redemption.

My restoration.

I'd have missed out on her if I had left that first day.

She was the fucking queen of hearts, and she reeled me in. She hadn't planned to seduce me, she'd said to Cap. She has no idea how tempting she is.

Slowly, my shoulders lower and I place my forehead on the steering wheel.

"Fuck," I whisper to myself.

A sharp rap on the driver's side window has me lifting my head and turning toward the person distorted by the fog on the glass.

I press the button to lower the window and stare at Cap.

"You stuck?"

Am I? Metaphorically, I don't want to move backwards. I don't want to be the grumpy, grouchy guy I was before Pear was in my life.

"I haven't tried to reverse yet," I admit, still clutching the steering wheel with white-knuckled fingers.

"I'll help you shovel yourself out."

A snow shovel rests in each of Cap's hands. If it weren't for the blunt blade, I'd worry he'll hit me over the head with it and then try to dig my grave.

Keeping the engine running on the truck, I step out of the cab and take the shovel he offers me. I don't speak as I sink into the deep snow again. I don't know what to say to him.

I defiled his daughter, who isn't innocent or youthful, but a fucking temptress.

We work in silence. Him digging along the side of my truck; me digging out behind it, making a path to the singular strip plowed up the drive so I can back out of my parked spot. So I can return to my life.

Cap eventually clears his throat once we have a decent trench of snow removed around my pickup. He sets his hand on the shovel handle, extending his arm as he stares at our work.

"She gave me an abbreviated version of what happened. All that you did over the past twelve days."

I squint toward the barn, not wanting to meet his hard gaze. "We lost power yesterday. Didn't actually complete all my tasks." I purse my lips. The tasks *she* assigned me, not Cap.

As I side-eye him, I see him nod, his gaze aimed in the same direction as mine. The owl house we'd hung on the eastern side of the barn.

"You took care of her these past twelve days."

I choke, before realizing he doesn't mean sexually.

"Kept her warm and safe." Cap lowers his head. "That's all I ever wanted for my girls. And for the men in their lives, if men came into them."

I don't respond. Pear clearly didn't explain how I rubbed a snowball into her neck and took her on a cold snowmobile ride. Then I recall both instances. How she squealed and laughed. How it felt to hold her on that day I attacked her with snow and then she held me on our snow-path journey.

"She's telling me I should give you one more chance."

I nod, sheepishly glancing at him before glancing away. I hear the *but* he isn't saying. He was done with me. He'd been correct. I'd been late to the last chance he was giving me. I fucked that up. That's on me. Owning my mistakes, as Pear explained to her father.

But what mistakes had she made? So, she fibbed a little bit. So, she let me stay. What would I done if I'd gone home? Wallow in my loneliness because my kids were away? Drink too much, feeling sorry for myself that my ex found another person?

My *person* was inside the house behind me or so I thought.

"If you deserve another chance . . ." Cap pauses. "Don't you think she does as well?"

My head turns so fast my neck cracks after a night sleeping on a blanketed floor. A night spent loving a woman with my body but also opening my soul to her.

I wanted her to let me into her heart because she was already deep within mine. Implanted by a Dutch pear pie and moonlight kisses. Fireplace confessions and tent blanket shenanigans.

"She didn't tell me the truth," I remind him.

He tilts his head. "True. And I don't condone a relationship that starts on a lie."

Another *but* hangs between us.

"However, she had good intentions. She wanted to help *you*," he reminds me.

"She did," I whisper, my throat thick as I blink toward the owl house.

Valentine's owls, and pears, and cows. I stifle a chuckle. Where will she be on Valentine's Day?

I turn my head, staring at my captain, knowing the answer.

I want her with me. I want her as mine.

chapter 22

[Pear]

The tears fall once I'm in the shower, then I scold myself. I'd done this to myself. I'd lied and everything backfired.

I'd fallen in love with him and now he hates me.

With shaky limbs, I pack my suitcase, picking up the twelve days of letting loose I had at the farm. Dad will want to talk, and cleaning is an anxious habit. If I can't straighten out my life, at least I can straighten up my belongings.

When I head to the front room, preparing to pick up the reminder of yesterday, I stumble when I see the blankets are folded and set on the couch with the pile of pillows we used. Plus, the dining chairs are returned to their proper place around the table. Our clothing is conspicuously missing, and I glance toward the fire, re-ignited to a low flame inside the fireplace.

Dad probably burned the evidence of my transgression.

Suddenly, the front door opens, and Brock steps into the entry way. He stomps his boots before looking up at me, where I've frozen in the middle of the living room.

Our gazes lock for a minute.

"I'm driving you to Chicago."

My mouth falls open, but the front door opens a second time, and Dad walks in, clapping his glove-covered hands.

My gaze leaps to him. He glances from me to Brock and back.

"He said he's driving me to Chicago," I state but my dad doesn't look as stunned as I am. "Maybe I should stay." My nerves rattle within me. "We should talk."

Dad observes me a long moment before removing his gloves and shucking off his jacket. "I'll see you soon in Chicago."

What? I stare from one man to the next. My dad removes his boots and swipes off his cap, like he's settling in to stay. Brock remains standing by the door, fully dressed, prepared to leave.

"Gonna get your things?" Brock asks me, his tone a bit terse.

I look from him to my dad, who's fighting a grin. When he looks up at me, he shakes his head with an expression that says, *see what I have to deal with.*

The choice is mine. Stay or go? Hide my heart or follow it?

Turning back for my room, I quickly collect my suitcase and tote and return to the living room. Brock steps forward and takes the case, then heads toward the front door so he doesn't drip snow all over the floor.

I step up to my dad, offering him a hug and muttering, "What's happening?"

"I think I'll let him explain." Dad presses a kiss to my temple and pulls back, holding me arm's length away from him. His eyes are full of emotion. "You're a beautiful, intelligent woman. And I trust you."

He glances over his shoulder at Brock. "And I can't believe I'm saying this aloud, but I trust him."

Brock tips up his chin, a smirk twisting his lips. He doesn't look at me and turns for the door, holding it open.

I slip into my coat and boots and lead him outside. Once there, Brock opens the passenger door of his truck, setting my suitcase behind the seat.

Somehow, I'd missed that a plow made one sweep up our drive and back to the road in the distance, which looks relatively clean despite yesterday's blizzard.

"What's happening right now?" The angry tension spiraling around Brock is not reassuring me that I should ride anywhere with him despite my father's faith in his fellow firefighter.

"You're getting in the truck." He stands back and holds the edge of the open door, essentially trapping me from escape although I don't know where I'd run. "And I'm driving us back to Chicago."

"Is this wise?" I question.

"Don't think you're in a position to question things right now, snowflake. Get. In. The. Truck." While the words are terse, his tone isn't aggressive. Hurt maybe. Confused. Irritated but not frightening.

I climb in the truck, and he shuts my door.

As soon as Brock enters his side, my mouth falls open. "Can I just say—"

"Nope."

"But I want to—"

"No."

"Brock."

The cab of the truck is warm, the engine already running. Continuing to ignore me, Brock puts the truck in reverse and cautiously backs up.

"Fireman," I drone.

Brock presses the brakes hard. The truck jolts to a halt. His eyes close a second before popping open and leveling me with a smoldering glare.

"We're not going to talk. Not yet. I need a coffee. You need hot chocolate. Then, we're going to hit the road."

He's telling me he's mad, but he's offering to buy me a hot chocolate.

I'm so confused but I roll with it as we pull down the drive and enter the local highway heading in the direction of Chicago.

+ + +

Nearly an hour passes before I can't take the tense silence in the truck any longer.

"I'm sorry," I blurt. "It was wrong. It was deceitful. I don't know what came over me. And I'm sorry."

Brock doesn't respond.

"What happened with my dad?" They'd clearly had a chat outside while I was in the shower and then in my room.

"Nope," he snaps.

"Brock, at least tell me he didn't let you go from the department."

Brock twists his lips before scratching underneath his chin. He hits the blinker on his truck and pulls off the highway into a rest stop. Parked at the back of the lot, he shifts in his seat.

"Explain this to me." His eyes narrow and he rests his arm on the back of the seat. "You trick me into staying at the house. Give me twelve days of tasks. And *now* you're worried about me losing my position with the fire department."

Startled by his soft tone but confused expression, I take a deep breath before saying, "I was always worried about your position. After twelve days, I thought I'd be able to tell Dad you did all these things around the place to help him out and he'd forgive you. I didn't plan for more to happen. I just thought it'd be nice to have some company while Dad was gone. And if he trusted you, I could trust you."

"Or my balls would be chestnuts roasting over an open fire."

I grimace. "Yeah, well, that was a little harsh."

"What was harsh was hearing you tell your dad you were falling for me, but you haven't said that to me."

I stare at him surprised by the wounded expression that takes over his face. He turns away from me, draping his wrist over the steering wheel, and stares out the windshield.

"You know, if you'd only asked me to stay, I would have."

"You were too eager to leave. Then you demanded to stay."

He harrumphs, knowing I'm right.

"However, I should have told you, you no longer needed to."

We remain silent a second. The heater is the only sound humming between us.

Finally, he speaks. "I didn't do all those things for nothing, though."

"Dad said you are cleared with the department?" My voice rises, hopeful and relieved. Dad couldn't possibly fire Brock for my decision.

Brock turns his gaze back to me. "Has nothing to do with your dad. I'd have done those things for you. I'd feed you, by canning pears, and keep you warm, by chopping logs. Do anything you would have asked me, if you'd only told me the truth, instead of making me think I *had* to do those things. Had to do them for Cap, and the department, and myself, but not because you wanted me to do them." His gaze drops to my lips. "All you had to say was you wanted me to take care of you."

Did he want to take care of me?

"How do you ask a stranger such a thing?" I admit, lowering my voice, embarrassed again by what I say next. "I was lonely." I'd already admitted it but it's uncomfortable to confess again. And like I'd already said to him, he seemed lonely as well. I shrug hesitantly and fiddle with the edge of my zipper at the hem of my winter jacket. "I just thought we could be lonely together."

Brock continues to watch me, but I don't look up. I've opened myself up to him in more ways than giving him my body. Slowly, I glance over at him.

"I wasn't trying to seduce you. I didn't intend to fall for you. I just—"

Brock leans across the seat and cups the back of my neck. "I'm still mad at you."

Confusion hits at the same time his mouth does, kissing me on a rush that draws me toward him, desperate to keep our connection. His lips move, hard and possessive. Anger lashes from his tongue. His teeth nip my lower lip. The kiss is my punishment.

Only, I don't feel punished when he pulls back and sets his forehead against mine.

"You once tried to throw something at me." He chuckles as we both recall me tossing a wadded piece of sandpaper at him. "But I didn't see this coming. You threw me a curveball with what you did."

I swallow a heavy lump in my throat, blinking back tears of shame.

"So, in the future, if you're going to toss something in my direction, snowflake, I want it to be your heart. And I promise to catch it. Treasure it. Keep it safe. And never leave."

"What?" I whisper, unable to hold back more tears.

Brock takes a deep breath after his admission, then kisses my forehead. "Now you owe me."

"What?" I chuckle soggily, trying to process what he's said. *Am I forgiven?*

And he feels the same about me as I do him.

"I've earned twelve more days, and only one way to prove I'm all in with you. I'm taking you to my place and introducing you to my kids."

Holy Christmas gift. Not exactly what I expected him to say, but I don't argue. Instead, I say, "Thank you. For giving me a second chance."

Brock smirks. "My boss said you deserve it."

Dad?

Then he adds, "My heart wants one with you as well."

chapter 23

[Brock]

I wasn't kidnapping her. With Cap's blessing, I was taking Pear to my place. For twelve days, like I said to her. This was her penance. She owed me time, but I didn't want to feel like I was stealing from her. I wanted more days, and nights, learning about each other. She might need to grovel a little bit, but I'll be on my knees as well, licking up every drop of her apology. I'm not a perfect man myself, and one little decision on her part does not put her on the bad girl list.

While misguided, her intentions were still good. She'd done it for me.

When we finally reach my house on the northwest side of the city, my anger has dissipated. I wasn't half as mad as I might have appeared. More stunned. Maybe even a little surprised that she'd want me to stay when I'd come across as a total dick at first.

As for Pear, she was a bundle of nerves when we pulled up before my place. A two-story converted bungalow, typical of Chicago. I'd put a lot of work into the house, and I lived in a quiet neighborhood full of fellow firefighters, law enforcement, and nurses. This was my community. We shared yards, watched out for each other's kids, and held a block party every summer.

I wanted Pear to like it here.

She pops open her door before I round the truck. Once she stands on the sidewalk, I place my hand on her lower back, sensing her anxiety.

"Your house is so pretty." She stares at it in awe.

Pride fills my chest and I press a kiss to the side of her head.

"You're beautiful. And my kids are going to love you." *Like I do.*

When we enter the house, I'm pleased to find it clean like Ellie had promised. Both kids worked over the break to earn extra cash for college, and I had their schedules in my calendar. However, I hadn't checked it before leaving the farm. I was a little surprised to find them both home, but also relieved. I wanted this introduction to be quick and easy.

"Hey, guys."

"Dad," Ellie squeals, jumping off the couch and rushing toward me for a hug.

"Hey, Dad," Nick follows after his sister, leaning into me. The hug is short, more like a brief tap of our chests and a clap on the back. Gone are the days my boy lets me hold onto him.

Both stare at Pear, questions in their eyes. I've never brought a woman home before.

"Guys, this is Pear. Paradise Klaus. She's Cap's daughter. And she's staying with us." She didn't have a place to live yet, and Cap agreed she could stay with me. Not that we needed his permission, but I appreciate his blessing. Maybe she'll view the time as a punishment. Twelve days for my twelve, but I'm hoping not.

"It's so nice to meet you," Pear offers, holding out her hand but Ellie steps up to Pear and hugs her. Pear glances at me over Ellie's shoulder. My girl is a hugger, but this is also a sign she instantly approves.

"It's so awesome to meet you," Ellie replies, pulling back to give Pear space.

"Hey," Nick waves, before holding out his hand, shaking Pear's. He slides his hands into his back pockets next, a tell-tale he's nervous, maybe even crushing a little on Pear. His cheeks are suddenly red. "So you're staying here?"

"Well, I . . ." Pear turns to me.

I'm quick to explain. "She's staying." Explanation done. "Let me go get our stuff from the truck. I'll be right back."

I'm smugly proud of myself as I scramble out to the truck to retrieve our bags, but panic hits before I've made it back to the front steps.

What if she hates my house, doesn't like my kids, and suddenly feels trapped?

However, once back in the house, I'm hit with a well of emotions and top of the list is love. Nick has taken Pear's coat and Ellie is showing Pear around.

Nick is hanging Pear's winter jacket in the coat closet when he asks, "Where did you find her?"

"A partridge brought her to me," I joke.

Nick just stares at me.

"Never mind." I take our bags right up to my room without further explanation to anyone.

Pear is staying. In my room. With me.

Soon enough, my kids aren't going to be around for the next few months, returning to their colleges for the next semester. Then it will be summer, and they'll be home but busy. The time will go by too quickly, and I'll really be alone when they each graduate from college and move out, carrying on with their lives as they should. So, now is the time to do something for myself.

Pear was it for me.

For the next few hours, the kids get to know Pear a little better and I sense they love her like I do. We eventually order pizza and hang out before Nick asks to go to a friend's house, and Ellie needs to go to work at an ice-skating rink in the suburbs.

Once they are gone, the house is quiet and Pear stares at me from across my kitchen island, twirling the stem of her wineglass.

"I built this piece. It's a custom cabinet." I lean on the sturdy cabinetry, running my hands over the butcher block top.

"It's beautiful." Still, her eyes don't leave me. "Your house is beautiful. And your kids are amazing." Her cheeks flush before her gaze drops. "But what's going on here?"

I slowly grin. "I meant what I said. You're staying."

"For twelve days?" Her brows lift, questioning me. "Am I a prisoner here?"

I shake my head. "You're free to leave if you have somewhere you'd rather be. But I want you to know, I want you to stay."

"Why?" Her eyes widen.

"Because I've fallen for you. But maybe fallen isn't the right word because I feel more like I'm floating when I'm around you. A caged bird set free." I chuckle at myself and glance down at my beer bottle on the island top. "Corny, I know."

Then I gaze up at her again. "But those twelve days might have brought me true love."

"Fireman," she whispers as she watches me.

I shrug. "And I want twelve more days. Then twelve months, and all the twelves after that."

Pear blinks as I round the island before I cup the back of her head. I stare into those beautiful eyes that stole my breath the first time I saw her.

"You said you were lonely. And you were right, I was too. Let's be *unlonely* together, baby. One plus one equals one, snowflake. You're my one."

"You're my one, too," she whispers, the sound thick with emotion. Then she's wrapping her arms around me, tying me tight within her hold like ribbon on a package. I hike up so her legs ribbon around my waist as well.

Setting her on the counter, I stand between her thighs, placing my hands on her hips. *God, I love her hips.* "Look at me," I ask and when she pulls back to peer at me with happy tears filling her eyes, I admit even more.

"I love you." I sigh. "It might seem fast but—"

Her mouth shuts me up. Her kiss erasing any doubts.

She's my one and I'm hers.

"I love you, too," she mutters against my lips, a smile on hers before we're kissing again. Slow sucks. Lingering laps. Tugs and pulls, but never pushing back. Never turning back. We only have time before us.

Slowly, she leans away and rubs her hand over my shoulder. "Tell me what happened with my dad."

I sigh, tugging her tighter to me and rubbing my nose against hers. "I told Cap I could lose the fire department, but I couldn't lose you. I told him I wanted to keep you."

"Keep me?" she grunts, shoving playfully at my shoulder. I only tighten my hold on her hips before slipping my arms around her lower back.

"I figured it might be a little soon to ask him if I could marry you one day."

Pear blinks. Maybe I've stunned her into silence, but I want to be clear where I want us to go. No deception between us.

With her arms looped around my neck and her fingers playing with the hair on the back of my head, she's quiet.

"What do you think, Pear?" Am I wrong in my assumption we're on the same path? Have I jumped to far forward too fast, like I said.

"If you play your cards right . . ." She fiddles with the back of my collar. "You never know." However, the gleam in her eye tells me she'll be saying yes when I officially ask.

"Speaking of cards." I pull two out of my back pocket and lay them on the counter beside her.

Pear turns her head and laughs. "The queen of diamonds and king of clubs."

"Souvenirs of this time I went to a pear farm for a twelve-day sentence."

Pear lifts her head and smiles. "Oh, yeah, and what happened?"

"Met a woman I love to kiss and fell in love."

Her smile turns into a beautiful grin, and she leans toward me.

"Funny, I met a man on a pear farm and fell into love, too. And now, I want him to give me all the kisses."

I happily oblige.

+ + +

L.B. DUNBAR

Thank you for taking the time to read GROUCH-ish.

Please consider writing a review on major sales channels where ebooks
and paperbacks are sold and discussed.

Want to know if Valentine's cows, owls, and pears are a thing?
Read Brock and Pear's First Valentine here.

Grouch-ish BONUS

Next up in the HOLIDAY HOTTIES: ELF-ish.
A fake relationship, millionaire-grinch, only one bed holiday romance.

Turn the page for a sample.

If you like firefighter romances, you might also enjoy
THE SEX EDUCATION OF M.E.
When a widowed professor decides dating is back in the books, her
new neighbor - a silver fox fireman - volunteers to school her in
rekindling a flame between the sheets.

OR TRY

STERLING BRICK
When high school lovers reunite twenty-years later while locked in the
men's bathroom during a funeral, this silver fox fireman is set on
reigniting their old flame.

Elf-ish

1

[Angelica]

"Possible heart attack. Ashford's. Eighth floor."

When the call came through dispatch, I was eager to take the ride. Alongside my ambulance driving partner, I wiggled in my seat at the prospect of entering Ashford's iconic department store located in the middle of the pulsing beat of retail in downtown Chicago.

However, I understood my assignment.

I'd be entering the building to save the life of the owner.

Jude Ashford is a bit of a novelty. At twenty-something, he inherited his great-grandfather's retail mecca which had been reduced to one flagship store after decades of being a major department store chain with multiple locations throughout the world. Everyone knows how the old man left his heritage—the original store—out of any buyout arrangements and willed the place to his great grandson, who by thirty-something had turned the seven stories into a glorious shopping destination.

Not that the place hadn't been great prior to Jude's rule. As a child, my grandmother would make the entire family dress up in our church-going clothes for a special dinner in the Oak Room, where we'd sit underneath a two-story tree that sparkled and glittered beneath the low lights of the dark-paneled dining space. On other occasions, she'd take us to a formal breakfast with Santa, often themed with holiday bears or popular children's stories. A highlight of any visit was viewing the windows along State Street that told a story through automated marionettes.

For me, I loved just standing on the first floor, adorned in bright red carpet, and staring up the middle of the store, where six higher floors were surrounded by gilded gold railings and the ceiling seven stories up offers a dream-like glass canopy.

Today, I wouldn't have time to stop and gaze.

Once parked beside the store, Maddix and I raced through the main floor, guiding a stretcher through the Black Friday doorbuster crowds, until we reached the elevator bank that will take us to the executive level.

A small group of employees are gathered outside the owner's office.

"Let us through," Maddix hollers, forcing people to part like the Red Sea.

Inside the office, we find a man in partial dress, slumped in a high-backed office chair behind a massive wooden desk. With his face ashen and his eyes wide, his slurred speech is actually a good sign.

"Not a woman," he moans.

I am used to this kind of thing. Older gents bitter that women hold once predominantly male positions, such as first responders. Men threatened by the strength and confidence of a female in such roles. I might be average height, but I am solid and curvy. My uniform isn't flattering to my form, but it isn't meant to be. The less attention I drew to myself the better sometimes.

And thus, I ignore *this* man with his white dress shirt unbuttoned to his waist, suit coat still on, and pants slung low at his hip, unbuttoned and unzipped. The hint of a tattoo along his side peeks out from the open clothing.

"I'm having a heart attack," he states a bit stronger to Maddix.

"Sir, I need you to remain calm." My glove-covered hand gently presses at the clamminess of his skin felt through the latex.

"Can you tell us where it hurts?" Maddix asks next, unstrapping the belt on the stretcher.

"My chest. My heart is racing." Jude weakly slaps his hand over a firm looking pec. "I feel like a vice clamp is squeezing my ribs. I can't take a deep breath."

Sounds like a panic attack, but I don't mention it.

Maddix stands behind the large, leather office chair while I move to Jude's ankles.

"On three," Maddix states before counting down, and we lift Jude onto the stretcher.

With a quick glance at a woman standing just off the corner of the beast of a desk, I have my suspicions about what caused his heart palpitations.

Being an EMT, we encounter the strangest things. Heart attacks induced by sex are not a novelty.

Maddix and I meet eyes only briefly, speaking a silent conversation we've mastered after years of being partners. Then, we hastily get to work administering oxygen, which our patient sluggishly attempts to remove while violently shaking his head back and forth.

With the cantilever finally over his mouth and nose, we've muffled his grumblings.

Next, heart monitors are placed against his chest. I typically don't notice the physical features of a patient. The human body is an incredible machine, and I've been conditioned to remove salacious thoughts about the flesh and bones making up a person.

But the beauty of Jude cannot be denied. Ripped abs. Smooth pecs. That side tattoo. And a smattering of hair on his chest. Not to mention a trail of darkness that leads below his dipping suit pants.

"You might have some drool there, Birdie," Maddix mocks me, despite the severity of our position, which is wheeling a patient to the elevator bank. Birdie is my nickname. It's a long story.

"Shut up."

Once locked and loaded in the ambulance, lights flashing but the siren not blaring, as it increases the anxiety of patients within the bank, Maddix picks up on a conversation we'd been having when the original call came through.

"So, you still don't have a date?"

"Now isn't the time for this," I groan, sitting beside our patient and checking his vitals, while Jude's eyes open quickly before closing again. His coloring still isn't right. He's almost putrid-green more than ashen. I don't know if I've ever seen this shade on someone's skin, but there's always a first.

"I told ya', I'd go with ya'," Maddix continues, skillfully maneuvering the ambulance through the day after Thanksgiving, early-morning traffic in downtown Chicago.

"And I told you, thanks but no thanks." Genuine gratitude mingles with my rejection.

Trey Maddix is a great guy and hot in the way best friends are *not*. He's good-looking to a multitude of women which makes him physically unattractive to me. He's a friend, honest and true, and offering to ease my suffering.

My *younger* brother is getting married in a few weeks during the holiday season.

Santa, stab me with a peppermint stick.

I love Christmas, but I don't have time for a family wedding, especially when the announcement triggered my well-meaning grandmother and aunt to ask when I'm getting married. Cantering why don't I have a fella, or a baby, or three, while at the same time, preaching independence for women and keeping your man in line. I can't keep up.

It isn't that I don't want marriage or babies. It just hasn't happened for me. That all-consuming, can't-live-without-you experience that leads to happily-ever-after and babies in a carriage. The kind of love my parents had.

I swallow thickly at the brief thought of my parents and return to the business at hand.

As the heart monitor begins to erratically beat, a wave of panic sets in *for me*. That niggling sensation I have within me right before things go bad.

And my patient crashes.

"Shit." On automation, I react, starting compression on Jude's chest, then checking his pulse. Repeating the motions one more time, I'm prepared to reach for the defibrillator but do something I've never done before with a patient

I lean down and press a whisper of a kiss to his cool lips. "Don't you dare leave me, Jude."

With another rhythmic compression against his firm chest, Jude gasps. Sputtering into the cantilever over his mouth, his eyes are wild and the iciest blue I've ever seen.

While I often find appreciation and liquid-filled relief in a gaze, these eyes are cold and frozen, glaring at me like saving his life was the devil's work instead of an angelic calling. A certain-something deep within me that likes to help others.

He moves his arm, limp and jerky until he reaches the cantilever over his face.

"Don't move," I warn, catching his wrist which is surprisingly strong while cool to the touch.

Ignoring my words, he grips the oxygen mask, moving it aside to offer a sliver of space. Then he grouses, "You shouldn't have. . ."

I shouldn't have what? Saved his life? Kissed him?

"But I did," I counter, stoic and without pride. This is what I do. The lifesaving part, not the random kissing thing.

He slightly shakes his head, but he doesn't resist me when I reset the oxygen mask over his nose and mouth. Instead, his frigid fingers wrap around my wrist while his eyes close. I assume this touch is a rare gesture of gratitude from Jude Ashford.

The well-known millionaire. The society playboy. The tycoon of retail.

Who at the end of the day, is only a man, albeit a selfish one

Continue reading ELF-ish.

ELF-ish

More by L.B. Dunbar

<u>Sterling Falls</u>
Seven small-town siblings muddle their way through love over 40.
Sterling Heat
Sterling Brick
Sterling Streak
Sterling Clay
Sterling Fight
Sterling Touch
Sterling Stone

<u>Chicago Anchors</u>
When your eyes are on the silver fox coach, more than the ball.
Elevator Pitch
Catch the Kiss

<u>*Parentmoon*</u>
When the mother of the groom goes head-to-head with the single father
of the bride.

<u>Holiday Hotties (Christmas novellas)</u>
Holiday novellas certain to heat the season.
Scrooge-ish
Naughty-ish
Grouch-ish

<u>Road Trips & Romance</u>
Three sisters. Three destinations. All second chances at love over 40.
Hauling Ashe
Merging Wright
Rhode Trip

<u>Lakeside Cottage</u>
Four friends. Four summers. Shenanigans and love happen at the lake.
Living at 40
Loving at 40
Learning at 40
Letting Go at 40

L.B. DUNBAR

The Silver Foxes of Blue Ridge
Small mountain town, silver foxes. Brothers seeking love over 40.
Silver Brewer
Silver Player
Silver Mayor
Silver Biker

Sexy Silver Foxes
When sexy silver foxes meet the feisty vixens of their dreams.
After Care
Midlife Crisis
Restored Dreams
Second Chance
Wine&Dine

Collision novellas
A spin-off from After Care – the younger set/rock stars
Collide
Caught

The Sex Education of M.E.
The original sexy silver fox.
When a widowed professor decides she'd like to date again, and a local
fireman volunteers to give her lessons.

The Heart Collection
Small town, big hearts - stories of family and love.
Speak from the Heart
Read with your Heart
Look with your Heart
Fight from the Heart
View with your Heart

A Heart Collection Spin-off
The Heart Remembers

BOOKS IN OTHER AUTHOR WORLDS

<u>Smartypants Romance (an imprint of Penny Reid)</u>
Tales of the Winters sisters set in Green Valley.
Love in Due Time
Love in Deed
Love in a Pickle

<u>The World of True North (an imprint of Sarina Bowen)</u>
Welcome to Vermont! And the Busy Bean Café.
Cowboy
Studfinder

THE EARLY YEARS
<u>The Legendary Rock Star Series</u>
A classic tale with a modern twist of rockstar romance and suspense.

<u>Paradise Stories</u>
MMA romance. Two brothers. One fight.

<u>The Island Duet</u>
Intrigue and suspense. The island knows what you've done.

<u>Modern Descendants – writing as elda lore</u>
Magical realism. Modern myths of Greek gods.

About the Author

www.lbdunbar.com

L.B. Dunbar loves sexy silver foxes, second chances, and small towns. If you enjoy older characters in your romance reads, including a hero with a little silver in his scruff and a heroine rediscovering her worth, then welcome to romance for those over 40. L.B. Dunbar's signature works include women and men in their prime taking another turn at love and happily ever after. She's a *USA TODAY* Bestseller as well as #1 Bestseller on Amazon in Later in Life Romance with her Lakeside Cottage and Road Trips & Romance series. L.B. lives in Chicago with her own sexy silver fox.

To get all the scoop about the self-proclaimed queen of silver fox romance, join her on Facebook at Loving L.B. or receive her monthly newsletter, Love Notes.

+ + +

Connect with L.B. Dunbar

www.ingramcontent.com/pod-product-compliance
Lightning Source LLC
Chambersburg PA
CBHW070501200726
48293CB00007B/2321